I0621422

Alyce Leaves Wonderland

Nataisha T. Hill

Published by TaiLorMade Books

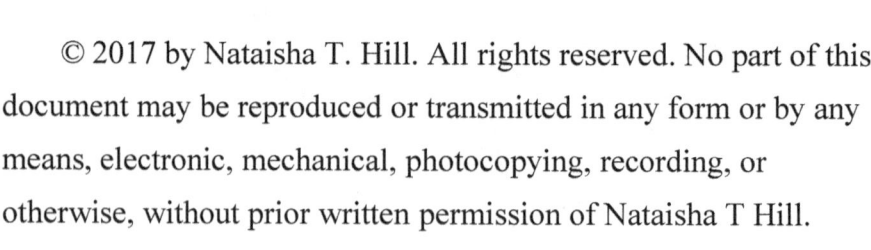

Chapter 1

"You are the most gorgeous girl I've ever dated, Alyce," Brad said, sitting down on the bed in the motel room he rented.

"Thank you, Brad," Alyce said, holding her head down as she blushed.

Alyce felt like the luckiest girl in the world as her mind began to wander off on all the great things she had going for herself. Her parents were very wealthy, and she was president of the student council, captain of the Beta Club, and in the top five percent of her senior class in her Virginia Beach hometown. She received an academic scholarship for her outstanding grades and would be headed off to college very soon. She was excited about graduating and going to the same college with her childhood best friend, Kelsey. Kelsey graduated a year earlier than Alyce and was also excited about her best friend joining her. On top of all that, she was dating one of the hottest guys in her high school class.

"Would you like some champagne?" Brad asked her.

"Brad, you know I don't drink."

"Okay, no pressure," he said as he wrapped his arms around her and gave her a soft kiss.

Alyce was enjoying the moment until she felt Brad reach for the zipper on the back of her sleeveless dress. She got up from the edge of the bed and walked to the opposite side of the room.

"Alyce, we've been dating for over a year now, and I've been respecting the fact that you are waiting for marriage to have sex. I'm not trying to sound harsh, Sweetheart, but nobody does that anymore."

"My dad said he waited for my mom."

"Alyce, I'm pretty sure your dad had other women he was having sex with until your mom came around."

"Even if he did, he still respected her wishes to wait until she was ready," Alyce argued.

"Either that or she had someone else pounding that cake other than your dad."

"You know what, Brad; I think you're being a jerk."

"Yeap, a jerk that's tired of jerking off. Look, I didn't rent this room to kiss and hold hands. I got a few friends coming by in an hour for the after-prom party."

Alyce looked at him with hurt and disappointment. This was the first time she wore contacts and used flat irons on her usually curly red hair. Even without contacts, she was still pretty with beautiful green eyes hidden behind her thick black framed glasses. She was about 5'4 with a curvy figure. She was normally shy, reserved, and had never had a serious relationship until Brad.

"I thought you said that you loved me and it was okay."

"Yeah, it was, but I figured you would put out since it was prom night."

Alyce grabbed her hunter green sequence purse that matched her hunter green dressed and walked out of the room. She remembered her dad telling her never to let a man see her cry. She went down to the motel lobby and called her mom to come and get her.

Her mom arrived about 15 minutes later, and Alyce hopped in the backseat.

"Well, that's a little rude. Do you want to tell me what happened?"

"No mom, I don't."

"Okay, well, should I even ask what you're doing at a motel, Alyce?"

"Don't worry, mom; I'm still the perfect little princess you and dad made me to be."

Without another word, Alyce and her mother, Gloria rode home in silence. Their relationship was complicated. With her athletic build and small frame, her mother acted more like a teacher than a normal mom. She couldn't remember the last time her mother hugged or kissed her. Her dad was her nurturer and constantly reminded Alyce how she would always be his little princess.

As a kid, Alyce frequently visited her grandparents on her dad's side, who were white, but never her mom's only surviving parent, her black dad. The only thing that Alyce knew about her grandparents on her mom's side was that her grandmother died when she was a baby. Alyce couldn't understand why her mother never acknowledged her dad. There were also rumors that Alyce had a half black brother, but she always dismissed them since her mom told her she was a virgin until she met her dad.

Alyce's mom kept her sheltered and rarely ever allowed Alyce to go anywhere but school, church, and home even though she had a car. Her prom was the first time in years that her mother allowed her to have some type of freedom, and even then, she wasn't allowed to drive to her own prom. Her mom said that she might fall into the peer pressure of drinking, so her not driving was an extra precaution.

The next morning, Alyce quietly sat at the breakfast table. Her dad had already left for work, and her mom was getting ready to go to her office job at a law firm.

"I think it would be a good idea for you to get a part-time job until you leave for school in August," Gloria suggested.

"My scholarship covers all of my expenses. Besides, I've been saving all of my birthday and Christmas money for the last four years."

"I know, honey, but you need a sense of responsibility, and I think having a job will help you learn how to manage your priorities."

"Well, I'll talk to dad about it and see what job he suggests."

Alyce knew that would be the end of the conversation. Her dad would never make her work. If anything, he would put more money into the savings account he had already started for her since she was a young girl. In addition to her dad's money, she had been secretly building a relationship with her mom's dad for quite some time, and he was also contributing to her savings.

She and Grandpa James started building their relationship once she got her license and her blue Ford Mustang that her daddy, Danny Wilson, bought her for her 16th birthday. She stayed at home by herself until her parents got off work, so most of the time she was extremely bored. She would normally go to Kelsey's house, but Kelsey was away at college.

One day she decided to look through some old childhood photos and found a document with Grandpa James' name, address, and phone number. She knew it might be a far shot since the paper was obviously old, but she wanted to see if the information could at least lead her to someone who may know him. Once she called the number, an older man answered the phone. She explained that she found the number in her mother's photo album and gave the man only the first name of her mother, just in case he wasn't her grandpa. Much to her surprise, he knew exactly who she was and gave her information to verify he was her grandfather.

After having several phone conversations with Grandpa James, they made a mutual decision to meet in person. Alyce was still a little apprehensive about meeting up with him, so they agreed to meet at a mall. Once she saw him sitting at the food court, she knew exactly who he was without him saying anything. Her mother was a splitting image of him. He was about 5'9 with a medium build. He had a paper bag skin tone with brown eyes and graying hair but was very handsome for an older guy.

She walked up to him, and he gave her the warmest hug as if she had been around him all her life. The more she spoke with him, the more she wondered how her mom could keep her away from such a pleasant person. His smile lit up the room as she told him about her academics and extracurricular activities. Although they didn't talk much about his life or her mother, she was excited to meet a part of her family that she never really knew. After speaking for a few hours, they decided they would meet up on a regular to catch up for lost time.

For about a year, Alyce used the extra two or three hours when her parents were at work to meet up with Grandpa James after school about once or twice a month. They would talk about her life, and he'd give her money for shopping or saving. Alyce had a million questions about his relationship with her mom. She didn't want to ask him earlier because she was afraid she would scare him off. By her going off to college, she would no longer be able to meet up with him as often as she did. She decided that the next time that they would meet, she would ask about their dysfunctional relationship. She also wanted to see if he knew anything about a possible half-brother.

Chapter 2

A few weeks after prom, Alyce decided to meet up with Grandpa James at a quiet restaurant about thirty minutes away from her home. It was always a risk of someone her parents knew seeing her out, so they tried to travel away from town, but close enough to get her back in time. They also chose different hangouts if they weren't hungry, such as the park or a small ice-cream shop. Grandpa James was very funny and could make her laugh at the drop of a hat, so it didn't matter where they met up as long as she saw him. He always made sure she was comfortable and had whatever she needed. Besides, Alyce was very witty. If she was questioned by her parents, she would lie and say she was out with her coach. For this particular outing, Alyce wanted something more private, so she could tell Grandpa James that she was going away to college and to get more information about her mother's life.

"Hello Grandpa James," Alyce said, embracing him with a hug before sitting down at the table.

"Hey Allie," he replied, using the nickname he gave her a few weeks after their first official meeting.

"Grandpa James, there are some things I've been wanting to ask you, but I don't want to scare you off. Would you get mad at me if I asked you about mom?"

"Baby doll, I could never get upset with you no matter what you say or do. I've lost enough years out of your life as is," he calmly responded.

"Well, that's kind of what I want to talk to you about, Grandpa," she said as she began to twist her fingers together. "Why wasn't I allowed to come see you?"

"Well…let me ask you this. Have you ever asked your mom why or talk to her about it?"

"Absolutely not! She would have a fit if she even knew we met up."

"Honestly, Alyce, I think when your mom has an idea in her head, it's hard to change it. I also feel that she thinks that she is protecting you by keeping you sheltered."

"That's what I don't understand. Why would she shelter me from her own dad?"

"Alyce, it's very complicated, but I will say this. Your grandmother and I loved each other very much, and with that love, we had your mom. As a matter of fact, you have the same beautiful, red curly hair as your grandmother did. You actually remind me of her in a lot of ways."

"Do you think I remind my mother of her?"

"I don't know, Alyce. People deal with losing a loved one differently and sometimes it's hard to accept the fact that the person is no longer here, so they lash out or blame others instead of getting the help they need."

"Well, I know that mom can't blame me for grandma's death, so it sounds like you're saying that mom blames you."

"What I'm saying is that things will happen in life beyond your control. You will wonder if you could have done something differently or changed your reaction to the situation, but altering the past is clearly impossible and just isn't how life works. Everything has a purpose, and if you believe in God, you'll know that he'll never forsake you. I know we've never really discussed religion, but you do believe in God, right?"

"Yes, Grandpa, but I wonder why God would allow part of my family to be torn in pieces."

"We're not in pieces, Allie. This is just a stage in life that we must endure. He brought you to me, right."

"Well, yeah, but it's like almost twenty years later."

"Better late than never, Sweetie."

"Yeah, I really didn't look at it that way."

"It's okay. There will be a lot of things in life that neither I nor your parents can show you or teach you. Some things you'll have to discover for yourself through trial and error. Just know that I'm always here for you and you don't have to wait once a month to call me. More importantly, make sure you pray about everything rather things are good or bad."

"That's something else I wanted to talk to you about Grandpa. I will be going away for college shortly, and I don't know how often I will be able to see you."

"Oh? What college are you going to?

"Georgetown University."

"Alright!" he excitedly exclaimed, giving her a high five.

"Did you go there too, Grandpa James?"

"No, but it's a great college for academics, and I know you will do excellent."

"It's about four and a half hours from here, so I figured I'd still come home on Christmas and summer break."

"That sounds excellent. I knew this day would be coming soon and I couldn't be happier. As a matter of fact, I have a little surprise for you.

He reached into his back pocket and pulled out his wallet. He pulled out a check that already had her name on it, but she couldn't see the amount. After he finished writing, he folded the check and slid it to her. Alyce couldn't contain her anxiousness as she opened it.

"Wow, Grandpa! This is ten thousand dollars!" she excitedly whispered.

"I was going to put it in your account myself, but I want you to be responsible. Use this money for books, gas, or whatever else you may need for college expenses. I believe in you and know that you'll do the right thing."

"Thank you, Grandpa," she said, getting up to give him a hug.

They spoke a little more before saying goodbye, and then Alyce left the restaurant. Even though he didn't give her a clear answer about his relationship with her mother, she believed him when he said he loved her grandmother. Alyce knew how overprotective her mother could be, so she probably blamed Grandpa James for something beyond his control.

After depositing her money into her bank account, Alyce drove home feeling confident about her future. Her four-year tuition was paid with her scholarship, she had a car to drive around campus, and Grandpa James gave her an extra financial boost, so she certainly didn't have to work. She could focus all of her time and attention on her studies and hang out with her best friend every once in a while. Once she opened the garage, she saw that her mom was home early.

"Would you like to tell me where you've been," Gloria spoke, not even giving time for Alyce to get into the door good.

"Mom, it's still daylight outside. You're asking me as if I'm sneaking in at night or something."

"I don't care what time it is; I asked you a question, young lady."

"I was at the library, okay. Now get off my back."

"Hey! Don't you take that tone with me in my house."

"Well, I guess I'll just use dad's portion of the house,"

Alyce said, walking from the kitchen towards the living room.

"Alyce, I don't know what's gotten into you or if you began smelling yourself, but you are still my child, living in my house, so you will obey my rules," Gloria demanded, following her.

"Okay, what rule in your mind have I broken?"

"You broke the golden rule. Thy shalt not get smart with thine mother."

"Wow, you're turning a pet peeve into a commandment. Classic, mom."

"You know what, Alyce, I didn't want to do this, but hand me your car keys."

"For what?"

"You are grounded young lady until you realize who the boss of this house is."

"Dad bought me this car, dad pays the bills in this house, so obviously dad is the boss, and you're his sidekick."

Without another word, Gloria slapped Alyce across the face. Alyce stood there with her hand on her face in shock. She knew her mother could get a little riled up, but she never expected for her to hit her. It was the first time her mother had ever been physical with her, so she wasn't sure how to react. She imagined herself running up to her mother and choking her until she apologized. She couldn't understand why her mother was so closed-off and unaffectionate. Even on her birthdays, her dad was always front and center at her parties while her mom stayed aloof, reading a book or cleaning the house.

"You've never loved me!" Alyce screamed as she ran to her room and locked the door.

About an hour later as she was texting Kelsey about the incident, she heard her dad arrive home. Kelsey came to several sleepovers at their home as a kid, and over time, even she noticed something odd about Alyce's relationship with Gloria. Alyce told

Kelsey in a text that she knew her mother was waiting downstairs for her dad, so she could tell her side of the story first. She cracked opened her bedroom door as she listened to her mother make herself sound like the victim.

Once Alyce heard her dad coming up the stairs, she quietly closed her door, hopped on the bed, and pretended like she was reading a book. Her dad knocked on the door, and Alyce offered him to come into the room. His tall, slender build was similar to a basketball player or a model. Alyce's dad was a very handsome guy, but the gray hairs throughout his low-cut curly hair told his age. He looked stressed as he sat on the bed and loosened his tie.

"Alyce, I want you to know that I love you very much and despite what just happened, I know your mom loves you, too."

"Dad, you and I both know that mom has never loved me. She's never done motherly things like bake cookies and cakes with me. She's never showed up to any of my soccer games or spelling bee's, or take me out so we could get our hair and nails done."

"Okay, but think about the things she has done. She buys you new clothes almost every week. She taught you how to make t-shirts, and put those holes in your jeans."

"It's called stressed-jeans, dad."

"Well, whatever it's called, your mother still taught you how to do it. We all have flaws, and it's important to embrace one another opposed to judging each other."

"Wow, you sound like Grandpa," Alyce said without thinking.

"Well, I was taught well."

Her dad clearly assumed she was thinking of his dad opposed to Grandpa James. Alyce was almost tempted to tell her dad that she had been spending time with Grandpa James, but she didn't want her dad to feel threatened by her new relationship. She never wanted to do anything that would hurt her dad's feelings and always wanted him to know that he would be number one no matter who came into her life.

Chapter 3

A few months had passed after Alyce's graduation, and it was time for Alyce's first day of college. She was so excited to be on campus with her best friend Kelsey that she could hardly contain herself. Alyce was slightly disappointed that freshmen students were not allowed to have a vehicle for their first semester of campus. The college administration thought it would be more beneficial for freshmen students that were staying in the dorm to familiarize themselves with the campus and their surroundings before tackling the hassle of driving on a huge and busy area. She and her mother hadn't spoken much since the slapping incident, so she wasn't surprised that her mother didn't come with her and her dad for her first day. Instead, her grandpa on her dad's side accompanied her on the trip to her new school.

Shortly after her dad and grandfather left, Alyce began to settle in her two-twin bed dorm room. It was twice as small as her bedroom back home, but Alyce didn't care. She was ecstatic about her new-found freedom. Her roommate hadn't arrived, so she took the liberty of choosing the bed that was furthest away from the door. They were not allowed to use nails, so she hung a few family pictures and posters of Channing Tatum to her wall using hanging strips.

After Alyce was done unpacking, she called Kelsey to see if she had settled into her new apartment. Since this was Kelsey's sophomore year, she and her roommate refused to stay in the dorm again. Dr. Fields, Kelsey's rich dad, paid up 12 months for their apartment. Kelsey didn't answer, so Alyce assumed she was busy. She considered calling Brad, but she hadn't spoken to him since prom night. She wanted someone to share her excitement with, but everyone seemed to be busy with their own situation. Besides, she had heard from other friends at her high school that Brad caught a sexually transmitted disease from one of the cheerleaders, so he might be too embarrassed to speak with her.

A few minutes later, Alyce was startled by the opening of the door. She felt a short rush of enthusiasm as she waited to see her new roommate. Alyce was shocked to see a short, black girl with long wavy hair step into the room.

"Uhm, are you sure you have the correct room?" Alyce asked.

"I'm not sure whether to be surprised or offended by the question. Do you have an issue rooming with a black girl or something?" she asked.

"Oh no, my granddad is black," she said, defending herself by pointing at one of the pictures her and Grandpa James took at the photo booth in the mall.

"Oh, so why are you so jumpy and tan then?"

"Well, my dad is white, and my mom is half white, so I guess I just got a small blend."

"Obviously. Anyway, my name is Jasmine, but my friends call me Jazzy because I love music."

"You don't play that loud rap music, do you?"

"Girl, what is up with you and all these stereotypes? If we're going to get along, you're going to have to lighten up."

"Oh, I'm sorry, Jasmine, you see my mom-"

"Yeah, yeah, yeah, your mom tried to erase the blackness out of her life by having a baby with a white man and the fact that your granddad isn't in any of those childhood photos probably means you recently met him."

"What are you, some type of voodoo girl from New Orleans?"

"Wow, your parents really got your mind twisted."

"Don't you dare talk about my dad. He's never said anything bad about black people, and as a matter of fact, he has black friends."

"Yeah, I bet your mom doesn't know any of them."

"You know what Jasmine; I think it would be better if you requested another roommate."

"Hey, I don't have a problem with whatever your name is, but you began your insults first, so I indulged," Jasmine said, beginning to hang photos of Denzel Washington and Matthew McConaughey on her wall.

As Alyce looked at Jasmine's wall, she realized how much her dad resembled Matthew. Not knowing what else to say, Alyce sat on her bed and started texting Kelsey. Even though Jasmine was very opinionated, she didn't seem as confrontational as her mother made black women seem. She canceled her text to Alyce and decided she'd try to work things out on her own.

"My name is Alyce Wilson, and my friends call me...Alyce," she said, trying to ease the tension.

"Nice to meet you Alyce and hopefully we can be great roommates," Jasmine responded, walking over to shake her hand.

"I couldn't help but notice that your poster of Matthew McConaughey reminds me of my dad."

"Wow, your dad does favor him," said Jasmine, looking closer at Alyce's photo of her dad. "He is hot for an older guy."

"Thanks. He and my mom have been married almost twenty years."

"Wow, that's a long time."

"Yeah, and they still seem to be in love with one another."

"Love can be so beautiful. I hope Gregory and I can stand the tests of time."

"How long have you guys been together?"

"We've been together going on three years."

"Is he going to school here as well?"

"No, but we promised each other to make it work."

"How far are you guys away from one another?"

"It's about an eight-hour drive."

"Wow, not to sound insensitive, but do you think he will cheat being that far away?"

"Chances are if he's not getting sex from me, I'm sure he'll get it elsewhere. As long as he doesn't get someone pregnant or give me an STD, I'll never know."

"What if you catch him out with someone on social media?"

"If that man is dumb enough to get caught, then we weren't meant to be in the first place. Besides, he's my first everything. My mom told me to have more experiences than just one guy."

"Wait, your mom was okay with you having sex with different guys?"

"Dating guys doesn't mean you have sex with them, Alyce," she said and laughed. "It just means she wants me to live life and see what the world has to offer."

Alyce knew right then that her mother-daughter relationship was completely different from Jasmine's relationship. She wanted to know more about Jasmine's relationship with her mother, but she knew it was too soon to ask too many personal questions. As outspoken as Jasmine was, she also seemed open-minded and friendly, not bitchy as her mother described most black women. Whenever Alyce's mom would snap at her, she was always tempted to ask was that her black or white side emerging, but she never did.

"They have a freshmen greeting tonight at the student lounge center. Do you want to come with?" Jasmine asked.

"Uh, sure," replied Alyce. "Do you know if they are going to be serving snacks? I'm starving."

"I'm not sure, but we can walk down to the cafeteria to grab something beforehand if you'd like."

"That'll be awesome. Let me grab my things."

Just as Alyce and Jasmine were getting their things together, they were both startled by a sudden knock at their door. Jasmine slightly opened it and saw a tall, slender brunette at the door with short, wavy hair.

"Is this Alyce's room?" asked the girl.

"Yes, this is our room. How can we help you?"

"I'm sorry. Where are my manners? My name is Kelsey. I'm Alyce's best friend."

"Kelsey!" Alyce yelled, opening the door widely to let in her friend and give her a welcoming hug.

"I see you two are settling in well in your quaint little room with your sexy little posters," Kelsey said as she sat down on Alyce's bed.

"Really, Kelsey? Could you be any more condescending?"

"Look, I understand you can't pick your room, but posters Alyce, really?"

"Alyce and I were just about to go and get some grub. You're welcome to come with us," Jasmine offered.

"Uh no. Alyce is coming with her bestie. We have a lot of catching up to do; besides, skipping a few meals wouldn't hurt since you've gained a few pounds."

"Here's my cell number if you need it, Alyce, I'm going to head out and let you two catch up," Jasmine said, grabbing her purse and walking out the door.

"Your roommate seems nice. How are you two getting along?"

"So, you're just going to sit here and act like you just didn't call me fat."

"I didn't call you fat, Alyce. I just simply stated that you put on a few pounds. Anyway, I have some friends I want to introduce you to, so let's go."

"Wait, we're not going to be out late, are we? Freshmen have a curfew."

"Alyce, you act as if I haven't already been here a year now. Of course, I'll have you back in time."

Alyce didn't want to come off as some spoiled brat or admit the fact that Kelsey's comment about her weight offended her, so she kept her thoughts and feelings to herself and agreed to go hang out with Kelsey. Besides, she and her bestie had a lot of catching up to do since it had almost been a year since they sat down and talked. Alyce hopped in Kelsey's black Audi that Kelsey's dad had bought her for her birthday. She hadn't talked to anyone about her breakup with Brad, so she was definitely ready to vent.

"So... you know Brad, and I broke up, right?" Alyce started.

"Oh, no, Sweetie what happened?"

"Well, he was being a real jerk after prom, so I ended it," Alyce responded, not ready to get into full detail.

"What a creep! I'd never thought he would take your virginity and then be a jerk. He doesn't even seem like that type of guy."

"I never said we had sex, Kelsey."

"Wait, you didn't have sex with your boyfriend of two years on prom night?"

"No, I wasn't ready."

"I don't understand."

"It's simple. I wasn't ready to have sex."

"What do you mean you weren't ready? You kiss and hug this guy for two years and then expect for him not to want sex on prom night?"

"Whose side are you on, Kelsey?" Alyce asked, clearly hurt.

"Look, Alyce, I know no means no, but you're not weighing your options. Brad is sexy, smart, and his dad is filthy rich. He doesn't even have to go to college, and his career is already set."

"Okay, are saying that means I'm supposed to give up my body because he has a promising career?"

"No, what I'm saying is you can't be daddy's little-pampered princess forever."

"Wow, I guess college do change people."

"Are you serious right now, Alyce? You're not a kid anymore. This is the real world where you have to make adult decisions without thinking about what daddy and mommy thinks."

"Thanks for your support best friend." Alyce managed to say holding back her tears.

"Alyce, stop taking stuff so personally. I am your best friend, which is why I'm going to tell you what no one else wants to say. Besides, you're going to give it up one day, so why not let it be with a guy you know well and has his life together."

"Right," Alyce softly responded.

She couldn't believe that Kelsey had such a shallow opinion about sex. To her, it sounded as if Kelsey was saying to only have sex with a guy who has lots of money. Something had changed her best friend. She wasn't the same girl that left her hometown a year ago.

Chapter 4

Alyce began to wonder did being away from her best friend for a year strain their bond or had Kelsey just gotten used to being around more mature women. Kelsey had cut her long, beautiful brunette hair, she was even skinnier than her usual 125lbs, and Alyce could have sworn she smelled cigarette smoke in her clothes. Either way, Alyce didn't want to ruin the long-awaited outing with her friend, so she sat back and listened as Kelsey continued to talk about her versions of keepers and losers.

About ten minutes later, Kelsey parked behind a row of lined cars in front of what looked like a fraternity house. Alyce had never been to one before, but she had seen a dozen movies with frat houses in them. She got out of the car and reluctantly followed Kelsey to the front door. As soon as she walked in the front room, she knew this was a terrible idea.

"You wait in here, and I'll go get us some drinks," Kelsey said, as she headed towards the kitchen. The music was loud, beer bottles were all over the place, and people were making out in every corner of the room. Alyce uncomfortably sat on the edge of a sofa next to two brunette girls that were slumped over one another. One of the girls fell to the floor, exposing her eagle tattoo on her lower back. Alyce was afraid to say anything to anyone, and with all the noise they probably couldn't hear her anyway. She was happy to see Kelsey return as promised with two wine coolers in her hands.

"Kelsey, you know my parents would kill me," Alyce said as Kelsey handed her a bottle.

"Alyce, stop being such a baby. Your parents are four hundred miles away. Do you really think that they are going to find out?" Kelsey said, ignoring the girl on the floor.

"Do you think we should tell someone that she's passed out?" Alyce asked.

"Alyce, she's an adult, and we're not babysitters. Besides, this happens all the time. She'll be right back tomorrow. Now, drink up, bestie."

Alyce thought about it for a minute and took a sip. She was actually kind of tired being Miss Goody Two Shoes. She was finally away from her strict mother, and it was time for her to loosen up a little. She toasted with Kelsey and drank the rest of her bottle.

After another drink, Kelsey took Alyce outside toward the bun fire where there were dozens of other college students talking and listening to music. A separate crowd was surrounding a guy under a gazebo playing a guitar.

Everyone seemed as if they were in good spirits and having a great time. Kelsey and Alyce walked over to an isolated patio set where Kelsey introduced her to her boyfriend, Matthew. They had briefly spoken about him on the phone, but this was the first time Alyce had met him in person.

"Wow, so this is the famous Alyce from Wonderland, huh? Your friend is even more beautiful than you described," said Matthew.

"Thanks," Alyce replied, not pleased with his Wonderland reference.

Matthew was extremely handsome. He was tall with jet black hair, tan skin, and mysterious bluish green eyes. His stare was so intense that Alyce had to look away when he spoke.

"Alyce, I wanted to introduce you to Matthew's cousin, Jacob," Kelsey said, motioning to someone in the crowd.

A few seconds later, a light-complexioned guy in jeans and a hooded shirt began to approach them slowly. He was medium height with nice broad shoulders and slightly bow-legged legs. He appeared to be very popular amongst his peers as he continued to get distracted on his way over to them.

"Is that your real cousin?" Alyce asked.

"Well, he is alive and in the flesh, so I guess he's pretty real," remarked Matthew.

"What I meant is-"

"He's black, and I'm white?" interrupted Matthew.

"Babe, didn't we already have this talk. Now stop giving my friend a hard time."

"I'm just joking with her, Kelsey, dang. Stop having a cow. My uncle is married and has been married to his lovely African American wife for twenty-five years. They have four children together, but Jacob is not only my cousin, he's more like a brother."

"I wasn't trying to offend anyone. I was just curious, that's all."

"You know what they say, Alyce, curiosity killed the cat," Matthew added, pulling a cigarette out of his pack and putting it in his mouth.

Kelsey began to giggle as she whispered in Matthew's ear. Alyce wasn't sure how she felt about her best friend's new boyfriend. He was very passive aggressive, and it seemed as if he carried a chip on his shoulder. He did compliment her in the beginning, so maybe she came off the wrong way when she asked about his biracial cousin. This was her first time being around older college students, so she decided not to press the issue.

"Hey, guys, what's going on?" Jacob asked, finally making his way over to the group.

"About time you made it over here, man. I thought I was going to have to come rescue you," teased Matthew.

"Y'all stop. You guys are going to embarrass me in front of this lovely young lady."

"Jay, this is Alyce, the friend Kelsey was telling us about."

"Oh, hello, Alyce. It's a pleasure to finally meet you. Kelsey has told us so many great things about you."

"Nice to meet you two as well."

"The pleasure is all mines," responded Jacob, reaching for the beer that Matthew pulled from the cooler.

Matthew gave Jacob some type of head signal and then whispered in Kelsey's ear. A few seconds later, Matthew got up and grabbed Kelsey's hand. She quickly finished her beer and followed him.

"Wait, you're not leaving, are you?"

"Alyce, do you really think I'd leave you somewhere you've never been before? Matthew and I need some alone time together, and this will give you and Jacob time to get to know one another."

Alyce felt neglected as she watched her friend go back inside the house and leave her outside with a total stranger.

"Are you excited about your first year here?" Jacob asked, sitting down and trying to change her mood since he noticed her discomfort.

"I am. I guess I'm just trying to get adjusted to a different world," Alyce admitted, feeling out of place.

"Yeah, I understand. It was hard for me to leave my brothers and sisters. I assume it would be just as hard for an only child."

"Wow, did Kelsey tell you guys my whole life story?"

"Of course not," he laughed. "She just mentioned good things about you."

"Like what?"

"She said that you were very smart and graduated at the top of your class and we might have a lot in common."

"What is the thing that she said we'd have in common?"

"She said we both enjoy crime and sci-fi movies."

"Did she mention anything about my parents?" Alyce asked, fishing for more details.

"Well, I didn't want to get too personal, but Kelsey did mention your mom being biracial."

"I figured she would."

"Oh, I apologize. I didn't mean to bring up a sensitive subject."

"Oh no, it's okay. Mom kept me sheltered from most of her family for some reason. I actually didn't get a chance to meet the black side of my family until recently. I connected with my grandfather, and he's an awesome guy. My mom doesn't know, but my grandpa said other family members are dying to meet me. Matthew mentioned you also have a black mom and a white dad."

"Yeah, I think it's pretty cool to have the best of both worlds. I definitely think you should take the time to meet the rest of your family."

"I believe I should as well and ignore all the negative things I heard when I was growing up."

"Yeah, people can be very ignorant when it comes to interracial relationships, but everyone's heart, which is one of the main organs in the body, is the same color, so why should we care about a skin pigment that has no legitimate function."

Alyce was very impressed by Jacob's way of thinking. The more he talked, the happier she was about Kelsey introducing them. He was opened-minded about everything and didn't get offended when she asked him questions about his black heritage. Even when Jacob's other friends came over to try and steal him away, he continued to sit with her and keep her company. The few times he did get up and leave it was briefly.

He told her funny stories about his childhood and what it was like to have several siblings. He also told her how he and Matthew didn't get along when they were kids, but they developed an inseparable relationship after the death of Matthew's mother.

"I know it's probably getting late, do you need me to take you back to your dorm?"

"Wow, I guess I lost track of time. Kelsey should be on her way back by now. I'll text her."

Alyce was having such a great time with Jacob that she hadn't noticed two hours had already passed since Kelsey left. She sent Kelsey a text to let her know she was ready to leave, but she didn't receive a response. She walked to a quieter spot on the side of the house to call her, but there was no answer. Not only was she getting frustrated, she was now getting worried. She walked back over to Jacob who appeared to be texting someone on his phone.

"Did you get in touch with Matthew?"

"I did. He said that he and Kelsey split up about an hour ago. She told Matthew she was too drunk to drive, so he drove her home in her car and had someone to come pick him up."

"I don't understand why Kelsey wouldn't text or call me to let me know that she wasn't coming back."

"She probably got so wasted that she forgot. Matthew has been very concerned with her drinking lately, but I guess he didn't want to bring it up in front of everyone. Besides, she knows I'm a trustworthy guy, and I wouldn't let anything happen to her best friend."

"It just doesn't feel right," Alyce said.

"Look, I know we just met, and you may not feel comfortable riding with me. I will call and pay for you a taxi or an Uber driver to get you back home safely," Jacob offered.

Kelsey had Jasmine's number, but she wasn't even sure if her new roommate was still awake. Besides, Jasmine was a freshman like her, so she didn't have a car, and she had practically ditched Jasmine earlier, so Alyce didn't feel comfortable reaching out to her this late.

"I'm going to call Alyce's parents and let them know to contact the police if she doesn't return their call," threaten Alyce.

Alyce felt that Kelsey would never completely abandon her. The least Kelsey would do is call and tell her that she was going home and call herself a taxi. However, Kelsey had been acting differently from her usual self. Then there was the fact that Matthew's sparkling personality didn't make matters any better. What if Matthew did something terrible to her friend? What if he allowed Kelsey to drink herself into a coma? Even worse, what if he killed her?

Chapter 5

Alyce picked up the phone to call Kelsey's parents to let them know that Kelsey wasn't responding. As soon as she began to dial the number, she received a text from Kelsey. Alyce canceled her call and read Kelsey's message that stated she was sorry for leaving her at the party, but she thinks someone put something in her drink because she had gotten very sick. She promised to call Alyce in the morning and left the hash tag *#myred*. That was a nickname that Kelsey gave Alyce when they were little kids, and Kelsey was the only person who used it. A huge relief overcame Alyce as she locked her phone and apologized to Jacob for being so paranoid. He told her that he understood and that he would have been the same way if he were in her shoes. She let down her guard and accepted the offer for him to take her back to her dorm.

Once they walked over to Jacob's green Toyota truck, she asked him if he could go grab a soda or water, so she could take her allergy medicine. Alyce closely watched as he disappeared into the crowd. This cynical idea gave her the time to take a picture of the truck and the license plate. Even though Jacob didn't come off as a criminal of any sort, Alyce wanted to take precautions just in case her perception about him was wrong. After she quickly snapped the pictures using her cell phone, she stood by his passenger door and waited for him to come back with the drink.

"All they had was Gatorade. Is this okay?" he asked, returning three minutes later.

"Sure, I really appreciate it," replied Alyce, moving over as he opened the door for her.

While riding back, Alyce noticed a Walgreens and a gas station that she and Kelsey had passed on the way to the party, which made her more relaxed. She noticed that Jacob was a lot quieter alone in the car with her and wasn't acting like the outgoing person he was at the party. She began to wonder had she offended him when she threatened to call Kelsey's parents. He said it was okay, but it didn't seem like he meant it. A few minutes later, they pulled up in front of her campus dorm as he turned down his radio.

"I'm sorry things didn't turn out the way you probably expected it to."

"It's okay. You didn't plan for my best friend to get drunk and leave me stranded."

"I will say this. I got to know a pretty awesome person that I wouldn't mind getting to know more."

"I think I'd like that," she said, pulling out her phone.

"My number is 555-1432. I work at a factory in the mornings, and I take night classes at a community college, but you can text or call me anytime," he offered.

"Great. I guess I'll see you around."

"I hope so," he said, adding a charming grin.

Alyce got out of the car and looked at the time on her phone. It was five minutes until the 11 o'clock curfew, so she jogged up to her room.

"Wow, you made it in by the grace of God," Jasmine said, lying in bed with a book in her hand.

"I know. You wouldn't believe what happened to me tonight."

"Let me guess. Your best friend took you to a wild party and left you hanging."

"You're starting to scare me," admitted Alyce, not expecting her response.

"Come on, Alyce. Your friend seems like the total party girl, and you're clearly the opposite. She probably only took you there because some guy needed a girl to hang out with his loser friend."

"How many friends do you have, Jasmine?"

"Goodnight, Alyce."

After getting herself together, Alyce turned off her light and got in the bed as well. She couldn't help but think about Jacob and the butterflies he gave her in her stomach. He was the total opposite of Brad in every way. He was thoughtful, understanding, and not judgmental. She wondered if she should text him to see if he made it home safe.

Now that she thought about it, where was home for Jacob? She was hoping that he didn't live with Matthew since Matthew gave her bad vibes at the party. *Curiosity killed the cat. Who does he think he is*, she thought?

Discarding Matthew's foolery, Alyce's mind wandered off into a blissful wonderland with Jacob holding her hand as they walked on a field of flowers. Mom and dad approvingly waved from the nearby bayou as she and Jacob laughed and kissed under the willow trees while butterflies danced in the sun's spotlight.

About five minutes later, Alyce found herself being carried away from her bed and put on the shoulders of two muscular men.

"Hey you guys, what's going on? Jasmine, wake up!" Alyce screamed, feeling frightened.

Jasmine didn't move. Everything around Alyce was blurry, and she couldn't see where they were taking her. Alyce tried to kick and move, but her body was paralyzed.

"Don't worry ma'am; your prince awaits you."

The men disappeared, and she spotted two glasses with a bottle of champagne on ice. The bottle was next to a private canopy bed sunk into the sand of the backyard of the party that she had just come from with Kelsey. She noticed that her nightgown was see-through and quickly tried to cover herself. She looked around but didn't see Kelsey or anyone else in the backyard.

"Don't be afraid my queen; I won't hurt you."

She turned around and saw Jacob exposing his six-pack abs as he gently grabbed her feet and began massaging them. The sensation felt pleasurable as he moved right along up her legs.

"Wait...what are doing? I don't know you."

"I love it when you roleplay my queen."

Before she could protest or say anything, he took his fingers and passionately began to massage her inner thighs and gently worked his way toward her upper torso. She felt her body quiver as he placed his hands on her chest and continued massaging her.

"Alyce, stop his hand before it's too late," said Jasmine, standing over the canopy bed laughing.

"What?"

Alyce woke up with her heart almost beating out of her chest. She looked around saw the pictures on her wall in her dorm room. She was in the pajamas she had on and no canopy bed or Jacob in sight.

"Wow, I didn't mean to scare you. I was just asking what time is your first class, so you won't be late," explained Jasmine.

Alyce couldn't believe she just had a sexual dream about Jacob. She was with Brad for two years, but she never had a sex dream about him. She wondered was she making noises. Even worse, she wondered did Jasmine hear her making noises. Alyce was too embarrassed to ask, so she went to shower to brush it off. The fact of the matter was that she couldn't. The dream was so intense that it felt as if it was actually happening. Ten minutes later, she came out of the shower with a towel wrapped around her body and her hair. Jasmine, on the other hand, was fully dressed and gathering her things together.

"How early did you wake up?" Alyce asked.

"Early enough to hear the passionate dream you were having," Jasmine snickered.

"Oh gosh, I'm so embarrassed."

"Alyce, you're human. Having a wet dream is nothing to be embarrassed about, Sweetie."

"Yeah, but this was different. It was something I've never felt before."

"Wait, you've never had an orgasm?"

"That's not what I'm saying."

"Okay. Excuse me for asking."

"What I'm saying is...oh, who am I kidding. I've never done it before."

"Alyce, are you saying you're a virgin?"

"Yeah, I'm still in a little girl's world."

"Girl, that is awesome. You should be happy that you have morals and values that you stand by and don't let anyone convince you that you should until you're a hundred percent ready."

"Where you ready the first time you did it?"

"It was actually my idea, but I did wait. I told Gregory from the beginning that I wasn't interested in having sex until I was ready and I felt that I was in love with him and genuinely felt that he was in love with me. I told him that nothing was going to change my mind and if he wanted to be with someone who was offering sex, then I was okay with being single. I stood my ground, and he respected that and treated me like a gentleman should. After about six months or so, I was madly in love with him and wanted him to be my first. It was a mutual decision that I don't regret."

"I was with my high school sweetheart for two years. I liked him a lot, and we had fun together but I didn't feel any passionate love. He was more like a best friend that I liked hanging out with and talking to on the phone. He dumped me on our prom night because I wasn't ready."

"Alyce, he's a total douche bag and clearly not the one for you. You're pretty, and you seem to be a very intelligent young lady. A man that isn't willing to wait for you is totally not worth your time."

"You think so?"

"I know so. Don't get me wrong. A relationship should start with that person being your best friend, however, if the feelings don't progress in a way where you feel you don't want to ever be without that person and he still gives you butterflies after months and years, then he's probably just that, a good friend.

"I never really thought about that way. Most of the girls I knew in high school were having sex for popularity or because the guys convinced them that was a way of showing their love for them."

"I can honestly say that my mom had several talks with me about guys and sex. She told me to respect myself first because if I don't respect myself, then how can anyone else truly respect me."

"Your mom sounds awesome. I wish I could've talked to my mom about boys and other girly things."

"I feel that the way your mom communicated with you is probably how her mom communicated with her. It's a cycle, and if you want to have an open relationship with your future daughter, you have to be the one to break that cycle."

"You would be a great philosopher."

"Speaking of philosophy, that's my last class today. I got to run. I'm going to grab me some breakfast and head to my first class. If you ever need to talk about anything, I'm all ears," Jasmine said, opening the door.

"Hey Jazzy...thanks."

Alyce was so touched by Jasmine's thoughtfulness that she almost cried. None of her peers had been so supportive about her being a virgin. She had just met Jasmine, but she seemed to be more nurturing than her best friend. Speaking of best friends, Alyce looked through her phone to see if she had missed a call from Kelsey, but she didn't. She didn't make such a big deal about since it was still in the morning, and she was probably still recovering from last night. However, Alyce wasn't sure what Kelsey was recovering from. Jacob said that Matthew claimed that Kelsey was drunk, but Kelsey's text said she was sick and someone might have spiked her drink. Either way, if Kelsey was conscious enough to text her, why wouldn't she answer Alyce's calls? Someone was hiding something, and Alyce had to get to the bottom of it.

Chapter 6

Alyce's first day flew by like a breeze, and she managed to finish all of her classes around 4p.m. College was an entirely different ballgame from high school. The classes were loaded with hundreds of different students of different ages and ethnicities, so it was impossible for the professors to get to know their students on a one on one basis. Alyce was so overwhelmed with finding her classes, listening to endless lectures, taking notes, and going back and forth to different buildings that she didn't give herself time to each lunch. Jasmine wasn't there once she arrived back to their room, so Alyce figured it would be the perfect time to call Kelsey, who still hadn't returned her call or messaged her, to see if she wanted to grab a bite to eat and chat. Alyce's call went straight to voicemail on the first call as well as her follow up call. It was unlike Kelsey to leave her phone off, but perhaps she hadn't charged it. Alyce didn't call Kelsey back but came up with another idea. Not talking to Kelsey gave her a good excuse to text Jacob and ask if he knew if Kelsey was hanging out with Matthew.

Alyce: Hello, Jacob. How r u? This is Alyce since u may not recognize my #

Jacob: Hey Alyce! Been waiting on ur call or text. How was ur 1st day?

Alyce: Great! Very Busy! I barely had time to eat :-(

Jacob: Sorry 2hear that. I cud take u out to get something if u'd like?

Alyce wasn't sure how to respond. She wasn't expecting him to offer to take her out. She would need to shower, do her hair and makeup on top of finding something nice to wear. However, she didn't want to turn him down in fear that he may feel rejected.

Alyce: I'm a mess, and it wud take me hours to get ready.

Jacob: Lol no prob. I cud bring u something. My treat of course.

Alyce: That's so sweet. U don't have to do that

Jacob: It's my pleasure. I'll text u a few nearby food joints n hav it 2u within 35min

Alyce was again impressed by his candid attitude. She wasn't sure if his aim to go out of his way for her was just an act, but she loved his personality and the attention he was giving her. He did mention that he came from a stable home, so perhaps his parents instilled in him how to be a gentleman. Perhaps she was getting ahead of herself, but maybe this was the gentleman like mentality that Jasmine said Gregory showed her. Although it wasn't an official date, Alyce went to wash up, touch up her eyeliner and mascara, and brush her flowing red curls up into a loose ponytail. She put some black leggings and a long, form-fitting shirt that showed off her curves.

About 30 minutes later, Jacob sent her a message to let her know he had arrived. He was already aware of the visitor parking areas, so Alyce agreed to meet him outside at a nearby picnic table. By Jacob knowing the campus area as well as he did made Alyce wonder did he have a lot of friends on campus? Perhaps he was the type of gentleman that brought lunch to several women.

She went outside and saw Jacob waiting beside his truck. He was still in his work uniform, so she must have caught him right after work. He gave her a huge smile as she walked up to him and gave him a friendly hug. He followed her to the table where he put down a large plaid tablecloth and placed the food on top.

"This is nice," Alyce said, breaking their silence as they ate.

"I'm just lucky I have the chance to do this for you," Jacob replied.

"Are you always this nice to women, or do you start nice and end up being bipolar or something."

"To be honest, I normally don't have time to date between my work and school schedule, but I feel a special connection with you."

"I'm supposed to believe out of all these women around campus you just happen to make a special exception for me."

"Well, rather you believe it or not, it's true. I think you are a very beautiful young lady and after talking with you for hours the other night, I know that you are also intelligent and have a lot going for yourself. A lot of girls around here are just in college because their parents said that they had to or it gives them a chance to be wild and be untamed. You seemed focused and dedicated to your dreams."

Everything Jacob said seemed so sincere. How could this nice-looking guy with ambitions and manners not be involved with someone? Better yet, how did his cousin miss out on the charming trait? As Alyce ate more of her food, her growing curiosity sparked questions about Jacob and Matthew's relationship.

"You said that you and your cousin Matthew practically grew up together, but you guys seem so opposite."

"Matthew went through a lot of changes when his mother died," Jacob said, putting his head down. "She was a very spiritual and nurturing mom."

"I am sorry to hear that. Perhaps you are the positive influence he's needed," Alyce responded, noticing the change in his demeanor.

"People deal with death differently. Some people can grieve and continue to rebuild their spirit while others get lost between the two worlds."

"I think that's what happened to my mom when my grandmother died when I was a baby. I think she lost her spirit."

"I'm sorry to hear that. Do you know how she passed?"

"My mom doesn't talk about it, but I remember asking my dad when I was like six years old, and he said a car accident. Afterwards, he asked me never to bring it up again because it would make my mom very sad, so I didn't."

"Matthew was around ten when his mom first got sick. He was his mom's only child, so he didn't have anyone around to console him when things got bad. He still has nightmares about some of her worse nights when she was in pain."

"Hopefully Kelsey will be there for him to help build him up when he's down. She's a very nurturing person, and that's part of the reason she chose to be in the nursing program."

Jacob didn't say anything else about Matthew or Kelsey. He continued to make small talk while throwing compliments at Alyce, but she could tell that talking about Matthew changed his mood. He thanked Alyce again for allowing him to meet up with her and said he had to get washed up for his night class at the community college. He promised to text Alyce as she gave him another friendly hug, but this time, she squeezed a little tighter.

"Hey, did you happen to hear from Matthew today? I was wondering had he spoke to Kelsey because I haven't been able to get in contact with her."

"Uhm…if I recall correctly, he told me they went out to eat. He said that she still wasn't feeling like herself, so he took her to his apartment so she could get some rest and have peace and quiet from her roommate."

Alyce wasn't completely satisfied with his answer, but she didn't ask him anything else. Instead, it left her with more questions. If Kelsey was out and about, why wouldn't she return her calls or at least send her a text? Furthermore, if she still wasn't feeling well, why didn't she go to a doctor to see if it was something serious? She couldn't interrogate Jacob because he had been at work all day. He was probably just repeating something Matthew had told him. Alyce went back up to the room to try and contact Kelsey again with no success. She decided to call it a night and try again tomorrow afternoon.

Alyce only had two classes on Tuesdays and Thursdays, so she was done with everything a little before noon. She wasn't focused in class from being restless thinking about Kelsey all night. She went back to her dorm room in an attempt to check on Kelsey once again. Once she made it there, Jasmine was frantic as she opened the door.

"Alyce, you are never going to believe what happened!"

"I kind of have something important I need to do, but what is it?"

"A girl that went to college here was found strangled this morning and dumped off in an alley."

Chapter 7

"What?"

"Yes, it's all over the campus news, so the dorm director moved the campus curfew up an hour," explained Jasmine.

"It happened on campus?"

"I don't think so. All I heard was that it was some brunette girl that was enrolled here. I think her apartment was off campus."

Alyce's heart dropped as she sat down on Jasmine's bed next to her. Her nervousness overcame her as she began twisting her hands in her lap. She couldn't get any words out of her mouth as she finally looked up at Jasmine and faced her with an awkward stare.

"Alyce, you're scaring me. Do you know something about this?"

"No, Jasmine. Kelsey won't return any of my calls or text."

"You don't think it's her, do you? Did something happen when you guys hung out the other night?"

"Well, not really. I mean...she left me at the house party and went off with her boyfriend, Matthew."

"Wait, she left you alone in a new place with a bunch of strangers and ran off with some guy?"

"She didn't entirely leave me alone. I met his very nice and courteous cousin who kept me company the whole night."

"So, I was partially right about your friend trying to put her boyfriend's friend off on you?"

"It's not his friend; it's his cousin."

"Alyce, that's not the point. You didn't even know this guy. How long did she leave you there?"

"Matthew called Jacob and said Kelsey got sick and couldn't drive, so Jacob had to bring me here. It's no big deal," argued Alyce, not wanting to tell Jasmine the entire story.

Alyce got up to go sit on her own bed. She was very frustrated with tears in her eyes. She knew Kelsey was wrong for what she did, but this wasn't the time to argue with Jasmine about Kelsey's motives. A girl was strangled, and she had no idea whether or not it was her best friend.

Jasmine followed her and sat down beside her.

"Now you listen here. I don't give a damn if it's three a.m in the morning or eleven o'clock at night. You call me if you ever need me or get put in any vulnerable situation. I know we just became roommates, but when you live with someone, you basically become family, and no family of mine gets into strange cars with strange guys. I can't believe she left you there by yourself!"

"Jasmine, I really do appreciate your sincerity, but my friend is still missing, and I'm here. Can we focus on what's important?"

50

"I apologize, you're right. You should call and see if you can get in contact with her. If not, I will explain the situation to the administrators and see if they would be willing to give us a current address for her."

"Thank you Jazzy; you're the best."

After Alyce watched Jasmine walk out the room, she made several failed attempts to get in contact with Kelsey. Alyce was tempted to call Kelsey's parents to see if they had spoken to her. She didn't want to alarm them since Kelsey wasn't actually missing, she just wasn't communicating with her. Surely if something happened to Kelsey, Kelsey's dad would've notified her dad. Not only did they know that Alyce and Kelsey were best friends, their dads belonged to the same golfing club.

"Alyce, I have good news," Jasmine said as she came back in the room. "There's a picture going around on Facebook of the girl, and it's not Kelsey."

Jasmine showed Alyce pictures of the girl's profile. The girl name was Amanda Schulz, and she was a junior at the University. A feeling of grief overcame Alyce as she looked through the photos. Amanda looked so happy, and she was very beautiful. Her profile said she was in the nursing program and there were several pictures of her with family and friends. Alyce continued to look at the pictures until something caught her eye. She came across a picture with an eagle tattoo. Alyce looked more closely at the picture and noticed it was the same tattoo she saw on the girl the night before at the party. What was even more alarming was that it was also on Amanda's lower back.

Alyce went to Amanda's recent news feed and made a startling discovery. Amanda was the girl passed out on the floor at the party. She had on the same clothes in her last picture post. A string of emotions overcame Alyce. She felt guilty for not listening to her gut instinct when she suggested to Kelsey to get Amanda help. What would have happened if she had gotten drunk with Jacob after Kelsey left her? What if Jacob happened to leave her there as well? Could she have been a victim, too? She wondered had Kelsey heard the news. Kelsey said that girls pass out at those parties all the time and showed back up the next day. Did she mean girls in general or was she specifically referring to Amanda? It was imperative that Alyce spoke to Kelsey as soon as possible. Perhaps Kelsey could have unknowingly seen the killer hanging out at one of the parties and could help get him arrested before he'd strike again.

"Alyce, are you okay? Jasmine asked, breaking into her thoughts.

"Jazzy, I have a confession to make."

"Do I need to sit down first?"

"Well...I saw that girl passed out on the floor at that party."

"Oh my gosh, Alyce, are you serious?"

"Yes! I wanted to call her a cab or get her some help, but Kelsey said girls passing out at parties happened all the time, so we shouldn't."

"Alyce don't blame yourself for something like that. Who's to say she didn't get home safe and the killer was already in her house or maybe this happened on her way to school this morning. No one really has any details, and that party was almost two nights ago."

"I didn't think about it that way. It would just make me feel a lot better if Kelsey would call me so I could talk to her about it. She may have known Amanda personally."

"If Amanda partied as much as you say Kelsey claimed she did, I'm sure a lot of people knew her, which may help with the police's investigation."

"You're probably right. I just hate the fact that she was so young and only had a few years to graduate. For her life to be taken prematurely when she was practically just beginning it hits close to home."

A few hours later, Alyce sat on her bed feeling lonely. Kelsey still hadn't called, and Jasmine went to the library for an upcoming group project. She wanted to talk to Jacob, but she vowed not to be the first one to initiate contact between them. She thought it would make her look desperate. Somehow in another dimension, Jacob must have been reading her mind because her phone rang two minutes later and it was him. He told her he enjoyed seeing her yesterday and would like to spend more time with her. Alyce liked him too, but more than anything, she wanted to take her mind off of Kelsey and the strangled college student.

Alyce was waiting outside when Jacob arrived and hopped in his truck. He had roses lying near his stereo console and handed them to her. Brad gave her a corsage on their prom night, but no one had ever given her roses. Alyce thanked him as she gently grabbed his hand and gave him a light squeeze. He returned the gesture by giving her hand a caress with his thumb that was so soft it sent shivers down her spine.

He drove them to a drive-in theater which was a popular hangout for students. They laughed and talked together as if the had known one another for years. He told her he had his own apartment near the community college and his job. He explained how he was hardly ever there and sometimes he allowed Matthew to use his place for dates. Alyce was just relieved to know that Matthew didn't live there. After the movie ended, there was a short moment of silence.

"Alyce, would I be too forward if I asked you for a kiss?"

Alyce wasn't sure how to respond. They hadn't talked about intimacy or sex period. He never tried to make any inappropriate move on her, and he had his own apartment and never once had he suggested she should come over. This made her feel comfortable enough to assume that he wasn't just after sex.

"I'm sorry, I shouldn't have asked," he said before Alyce could respond.

Jacob cranked up the truck and began to pull out of the parking lot. Alyce was slightly disappointed because she wanted him to kiss her, but wasn't sure if he assumed it would lead to something else. *A grown man with his own apartment would have to be sexually active*, she thought. As Alyce looked out the window wishing she had said something; she was distraught by what she did see. It was Kelsey parked in the back of the theater making out with a woman!

Chapter 8

Alyce was just as hurt as she was pissed. How could Kelsey blatantly do this to her! She couldn't believe that her best friend was purposely ignoring her calls. All this time she had been worried about her friend being found in an alley or something and her friend was out having the time of her life with a new friend. She began to imagine Kelsey looking at her calls and laughing with her new friends. *How could she be so thoughtless*, Alyce wondered. That's probably why she thought Brad wasn't a jerk because she was an even bigger one. Alyce knew she had less than an hour until the new curfew, but she was willing to take whatever punishment that came behind it. Kelsey had finally pushed her to her limit. She was ready to give Kelsey a piece of her mind.

"Jacob, stop this truck right now!"

He immediately obeyed as he pulled over to the opposite side of the back parking lot. Just as he was about to apologize again, Alyce pulled him by his shirt collar and gave him a quick sensual kiss on the lips. Without giving him time to respond, she got out of the car and walked across the driveway to Kelsey's door and banged on the window. Startled by the loud pounds, Kelsey raised her head up with a trace of a powdery substance underneath her nose and let down the window.

"Hey, what is your damn problem banging on my window?"

"Are you doing cocaine?" Alyce asked in a state of shock.

"Look, Sarah, its Ms. Goody Two Shoes," mocked Kelsey.

"Are you kidding me right now, Kelsey? I've been calling you for almost three days!"

"So, I didn't want to talk to you," replied Kelsey as her stoned passenger laughed.

"I've been your best friend since we were five, why wouldn't you want to talk to me? I've been worried sick about you and even more scared when they found that dead college girl earlier."

Kelsey put her head down as if a shred of decency came over her. Her hair looked wet as if she hadn't washed it in weeks and now, Alyce figured out why she was so thin. Kelsey clearly needed help, but from the looks of things, she wasn't going to allow Alyce to intervene.

"Did Matthew do this to you?" Alyce asked.

"Matthew?" Kelsey repeated, disgusted by the question.

"I've never seen you act like this until you met him."

"You know what, Alyce? You have some nerve judging people all of the time."

"I don't judge people," Alyce replied.

"Yes, you do," argued Kelsey. "You and your mother sit around all day turning your nose up at people when they don't fit into you guy's expectations when in actuality, your entire life is a lie."

"What do you mean my life is a lie?"

"Alyce, turn around and go back to kiddy land while daddy pats you on your little bottom and feeds you a bottle. You're not ready for the real world."

"You're snorting powder up your nose, and you have the audacity to try and insult me?"

"Do you want to know the real reason why Brad dumped you? Wait, don't answer that, I'll tell you. He said he didn't want to continue to date a mix breed mutt."

"Uh…Kelsey, maybe we should leave," suggested Sara, seeing the hurt in Alyce's eyes.

"No, this little virgin wanted to play in the big leagues, so I'm going to show her how it's done."

"If you have something to say you say it you powdered-nose demon."

"Really Alyce? Do you also want to know the real reason why your mom hates her black heritage?"

"Why should I listen to a powder-head?"

"Because your dad told my dad who told this powder-head that your grandpa Jerry, James, or whatever his name is killed his wife, aka your grandmother."

Alyce took a few steps back from Kelsey's car. Alyce never told Kelsey anything about her grandfather, not even his name, so there had to be some legitimacy to this statement. She wondered did Kelsey recently find out this information or had she known since they were kids. Rage came over Alyce as she watched Kelsey pretend to stab Sara as if she was reenacting what happened. She suddenly grabbed Kelsey by the hair and attempted to pull her out of the car through the window. Sara was so high and horrified that she sat there like a statue.

Alyce felt Jacob's arms suddenly wrap around her body as he softly whispered that they should leave. Alyce wanted to rip the hair from Kelsey's scalp, but Jacob's calm voice and gentle tug forced her to ease up and finally let go. Kelsey pushed her upper half of her body back into the car and looked in the mirror at her bleeding nose.

"You broke my nose!" Kelsey yelled, continuing to check out the damage. "You and I are no longer friends. You are dead to me from now on."

Alyce looked at Kelsey in disgust. Making her nose bleed was an accident, but she wasn't sorry. Her face must have hit the door as soon as Alyce grabbed her head. A couple of students nearby began to slowly emerge from their cars to visually investigate the commotion.

"Kelsey, we can't let others see the stuff," Sara said, reminding her about the cocaine on the armrest.

Kelsey quickly started up her car and put it in reverse. "Why don't you ask Jacob what happened to Amanda. He probably screwed her to death," she said and sped off.

Jacob immediately escorted Alyce back to his truck and left the parking lot. Alyce sat quietly on the passenger side trying to fight back her tears. Her adrenaline was still going, but she didn't want to show her emotions in front of Jacob. It was bad enough he had to see her yank her best friend halfway out of a window. She couldn't believe her first physical altercation was with the person she thought was her best friend. *Why would she say such hurtful things? Did drugs really make her that much of a monster?* Alyce couldn't help it. The tears started rolling down her face and nothing could stop the deep sobbing.

Jacob pulled over to the side of a Dairy Queen that was near the campus. He got out of the car, open Alyce's door, and gently pulled her up to embrace her with a hug. Alyce couldn't help but to hold on to him as she cried in his arms.

"I'm sorry, you must think I'm crazy," Alyce said, cleaning her face with the end of her blouse."

"I think you've been through more than enough in one night," he said, helping her dry her tears with a soft caress down her cheeks.

"Did Matthew tell you she would be there?"

"I haven't talked to Matthew since the day he said he and Kelsey went to lunch together. Besides, I would've told you first had I known about her whereabouts."

Is it true what Kelsey said about you and Amanda?"

"Alyce, that's a long conversation, and if we get you back now, you won't be late for curfew."

"Jacob, I really like you, but if you can't be truthful about something this serious then maybe we should just cut our losses."

"I dated Amanda months ago. Yes, I really liked her until she started dating Matthew behind my back. Once Matthew ditched her for Kelsey, she became irrational and jealous. To try and get back at Matthew, Amanda came to my apartment and tried to have sex with me. I was on my way to class, and I had already given Matthew a key to the apartment to spend time with Kelsey. They showed up and saw Amanda naked on my bed."

"Were you about to sleep with her?"

"I had already told her to leave several times, but she wouldn't until she was embarrassed by them showing up. I was completely done with her then, and I'm completely done with her now."

"Well, of course, you're done with her now since you don't have the option."

"I knew you had some cockiness to you under that beautiful red hair of yours," he said as he caressed the side of her face.

Alyce took a step back and squinted her eyes. Jacob was all smiles and didn't seem bothered by the fact that someone he had previously dated was dead. He also spoke as if Amanda was still alive. He had to have heard about it from friends around campus or on the news. Then it dawned on Alyce that Jacob was probably at work all day. Maybe he hadn't heard the news!

"Uhm…are you on Facebook or anything?"

"No, I don't have a need for social media right now. Why do you ask?"

"Jacob, I don't know how to say this or if you knew…but… Amanda is dead."

Chapter 9

"Alyce, why would you say such a thing," he asked, not sure if he believed her.

Alyce felt horrible. She had no idea that Jacob was personally involved with Amanda. Alyce felt that less guilty about breaking Kelsey's nose. She didn't want to show Jacob the updated coverage that was reported across the campus television later that day, but at this point, she had no choice. She reached into her purse to get her phone and pulled up the previously recorded breaking news segment. After watching, Jacob closed his eyes, put his forearm on the door of his truck, and laid his head on his arm. Alyce wasn't sure what to do or say. He said he wasn't interested in Amanda anymore, but surely, he didn't expect her to be dead. Alyce eased her hand on his shoulder and apologized. It was the first thing that came to her mind at that moment. He took a deep breath, put his hand on top of hers, and told her he had to get her home.

A few minutes later, he pulled up in front of her building and opened the truck door for her.

"Are you okay?" he asked.

"I'll be fine. It's just a lot to take in. Never in a million years would I have thought I would be dragging my best friend out of her car by her hair."

"People change in certain situations, and certain situations make people change," he responded.

Are you going to be alright?" she asked, wondering what was really going through his mind since he just found that his ex-girlfriend was now deceased.

"I'll be okay. All that matters is that you're safe."

He gave Alyce a kiss on the cheek and climbed back into his truck. Once Alyce was inside the glass entranceway, he drove out of her view. As soon as Alyce made it to her door, that was an envelope sticking to it with her name on it. She opened it up, and it read **Violation Notice**. At the bottom of the note, it said it was just a reminder since the temporary curfew had just changed today. Jasmine was fast asleep, so Alyce quietly washed up and got into her pajamas. She laid her head on the pillow as the night's events swarmed through her head. There was no way Grandpa James would kill his wife or anyone period. He was too easygoing and caring. There had to be some type of mix up or lies spread. Alyce wasn't in law school, but she was smart enough to know if Grandpa James was guilty, he'd be in jail. Kelsey and her dad were liars. She couldn't wait to call her dad tomorrow and get the true story, or better yet, she'd call Grandpa James and get the truth from him.

The following weeks had been a roller coaster of emotions for Alyce. She hadn't seen or heard from Kelsey since their fight and didn't care if she ever did. Kelsey was being controlled by the very thing that their parents forbid them to do. She wasn't sure whether or not if she was going to tell her dad about the fight. She knew he would immediately inform Kelsey's dad. Kelsey was the pride and joy of Dr. Field's life. Even if Dr. Fields did confront his daughter about the drugs, she'd lie and make her dad believe that Alyce was delusional. It could backfire even more by their dads becoming enemies. Although Alyce knew that Kelsey needed help, it just seemed like a no-win situation for her to help, so she decided to let life take its course.

With several felled attempts to get in touch with Grandpa James, Alyce also put Kelsey's allegations about her grandfather on the back burner. She decided a conversation with such a sensitive subject should be addressed face to face anyway. Besides, she was so overwhelmed with mid-term projects and test that she didn't have time for anything extra. To make matters worse, she still hadn't talked to her mom. Although they had previously had their share of disagreements back in the day, they had never gone that long without talking to each other. Deep down inside, Alyce really loved her mom, and all she ever wanted was to feel loved by her. She couldn't understand why her mother failed to see that. She tried to talk to her dad about it, but lately, his answers were always vague, or he'd change the subject every time she mentioned her mom. Although Alyce couldn't quite put her finger on it, something weird was going on with him.

On the plus side of things, Alyce and Jasmine developed a close-knit bond. They helped one another with their school work, they went to different events together, and Alyce even developed a mother-daughter friendship with Jasmine's mom through FaceTime. As much as Alyce wanted to go with Jasmine to visit her hometown the upcoming fall break, she knew she had unfinished business at home and plus her dad would be crushed if she didn't spend her break with them. Nevertheless, she and Jasmine remained practically inseparable.

Although Alyce's new friendship was thriving, her courtship with Jacob had taken a turn. After a few more dates, dorm visits, and finally revealing to him that she was a virgin, he began to distance himself. Their phone conversations became very brief and less frequent. He started taking extra shifts and worked an extreme amount of overtime hours. He'd still text her good morning and ask how her day went, but that was about it. He wasn't as eager to see her as he had been. Even though he said he missed her, he didn't make an effort to try and spend quality time with her. Alyce wasn't sure if he really needed the money or if he was trying to avoid her. Perhaps keeping himself busy was his way of trying to get Amanda's death out of his mind or maybe he wasn't interested in being with a girl that wasn't sexually active. Jacob was a very charming guy, and he seemed popular with the ladies at the party, so maybe he wasn't ready to be with only one woman. Either way, it left Alyce feeling somewhat alone and confused. She was going to need some straightforward answers from him soon, or she was going to move on from him altogether.

Jasmine and Gregory gave Alyce a ride to the airport since Gregory drove to see Jasmine. Alyce's dad had purchased her a round trip plane ticket back home. She had been on several plane trips with her mom and dad for family vacations and business trips, so she was comfortable riding alone. Besides, by the time the songs she had lined up on her playlist were over, she'd be landing.

Alyce really missed her dad and was excited to see him when he picked her up from the airport. As she expected, her mother didn't come along for the ride. She decided not to allow her mother's abstinence to bother her or stop her from her plans to have a heart to heart with her. Even though Alyce's dad seemed happy to see her, he was unusually quiet once in the car. It wasn't like him not to ask a million questions, especially since he hadn't seen her in a few months.

"Have you and mom been enjoying your alone time now that I'm out of the way," teased Alyce, trying to break the ice.

He tried to crack a smile, but he couldn't. Instead, tears began to roll down his face. Something deep was hurting him. Alyce even heard it in his voice when she spoke with him over the phone. She didn't know what to do because she had never seen her dad cry. He was always the stronghold of the family and gave everyone instruction. Seeing him vulnerable put her in a weird space because she knew something was terribly wrong. She knew whatever her dad was holding on to had already changed his life. She knew in return that whatever her dad was about to tell her was also going to change her life.

"Dad, what is it?"

"Alyce…something unthinkable happened while you were away. I couldn't muster the courage to tell you over the phone, and it's even harder to tell you right now."

Her dad pulled into their driveway and put the car in park. He rested his elbow on the steering wheel and put his head in his hands. Alyce turned toward her dad and put her hand on his shoulder.

"It's okay dad. We'll get through it together."

"Oh God, Alyce. Your mother is in the hospital."

"How? I mean what happened? Is she okay?"

"No, she's not okay…she's not okay. She tried to kill herself."

Alyce paused in a state of confusion. "That doesn't even sound like mom. There must be a mistake or...or someone is trying to set her up," she protested, "I want to see her! Let's go get her!"

"Alyce, calm down. You don't understand."

"No, dad! You're wasting time! Let's go save her."

Mr. Wilson got out of the car and slammed the door. He put his forearm on the hood, rested his head on it, and sobbed. It was at that point when Alyce knew whatever the situation was; it seemed hopeless. As Alyce slowly walked over to comfort her dad, she had a flashback of Jacob's reaction when she told him about Amanda.

"Why dad? Why would mom try to kill herself?"

Mr. Wilson rose up with tears steadily following down his face. "She...she killed her dad."

Chapter 10

Alyce wasn't able to process what her dad had just confessed to her. She was hoping that the tears and the story were all made up and he was trying to pull the greatest prank of all time. It didn't make sense. Why on Heaven's earth would mom try to kill her own dad after all this time? What kind of trigger could have made her want to eradicate the only parent she had left in this world? Then it dawned on Alyce that there was only one recent connection between Grandpa James and her mom. It was her! Gloria must have found out that Alyce and Grandpa James had been communicating, but how? Even if that was the case, what was so horrible about her getting to know her grandfather that would drive her mom to do such a horrendous thing?

As she stood there without any understanding of the devastating predicament she was enduring, she thought about her dad. He had to be going out of his mind. How long had he been holding on to all of this? Did he know the truth about his wife's family secrets or was he left in the dark like her? Furthermore, with her in college and mom in the hospital, he had no one. What was the status of mom's condition and if she somehow did pull through, was she going to spend the rest of her life in prison? As hard as this was for dad, Alyce needed details.

"Dad, when did all this happen?

Mr. Wilson let out a sigh of defeat. It was if he had the whole world on his shoulders and nowhere to place it. With his head down, he walked over to the front of his car and leaned on the hood. He remained silent as Alyce stood there waiting for a response. She knew he was trying to get himself together, so he could explain to his only daughter why her mother took her dad's life and tried to take her own.

"Your mother opened one of your bank statements and saw the copy of the $10,000 check from your grandfather. She was enraged, yelling about how she warned him not to ever contact you and how you betrayed her by meeting up with him. I tried to calm her down, but she was hell-bent. After a few heated phone conversations with him, she went to his home, they argued, and the next thing you know, she said she had a knife in her hand."

"Did she bring the knife with her? How do you just happen to have a knife in your hand? Did Grandpa James try to attack her or something?" Alyce questioned.

"Those are the only details she gave me. She went over there on a Monday, they found your grandfather's body the following Wednesday, and your mother confessed to me that she did it after it aired on the news that Wednesday night. She said she was going to get a lawyer and turn herself in the next morning. I tried to get some type of understanding or explanation about what happened. She said she couldn't talk about it, but she wanted me to know the whole truth, beginning from her mother's accident. That morning I went in the bedroom and when I tried to-," her dad was having a hard time getting his words out. "I tried to...to wake-,"

"Dad, just breathe and take it slow," Alyce said, trying to comfort her dad by rubbing his back.

"I tried to wake her up, Alyce, but she wouldn't wake up," he loudly sobbed. "The doctor said she overdosed on opiates."

Alyce put her arms around her dad and allowed him to cry on her shoulder. As much as Alyce wanted to sob with him, she knew she had to be strong for him. What was he going to do without the woman he had been with for over 25 years? How was he going to react when his social circles started asking questions and making accusations? She realized that her dad may need her more than she thought. Although she wasn't able to make a definitive decision, she considered dropping out of school for a semester or two or at least until she felt her dad would be okay.

Alyce looked around to see if anyone in the neighborhood was outside watching her dad break down. She needed to protect her dad in his vulnerable state of mind, so she insisted that they continue the conversation in the house.

Her dad sat down at the kitchen table while Alyce fixed him a glass of Jack Daniels on the rocks. It was clear that her dad knew just about as much as she now knew about the incident. It was also obvious to Alyce that her mom didn't talk much about her grandmother's accident to her own husband…or did she? Was her dad hiding something that he knew? Her dad would have to have some type of implication about mom's relationship with her mom and Grandpa James before she was born.

"Uhm…dad…did mom have a good relationship with her mom?"

"Why do you ask?" suspiciously questioned her dad as he raised his head from his glass.

"Well, mom never talked about her mom with me, and she was somewhat closed off when it came to having an open mother-daughter relationship with me as well, so I was just curious if it had something do with how her mom treated her."

Her dad took a minute to think about Alyce's response. "I believe that your mom and your grandmother were a lot alike in many ways. They were both stubborn and very opinionated, especially when it came to raising you. Your mother wanted to work on cars like your Grandpa James, but your grandmother said it was not lady-like and she should be a stay-at-home mom and focus on raising you."

"So, mom left her dreams behind to raise me. Do you think that's why she had a little resentment toward me?"

"I don't think your mom ever resented you."

"Mom told me you guys were poor in the beginning."

"Well, we weren't in the financial position we are now, but we made it work. After your grandmother's accident, your mom was left with a huge settlement from the insurance, so she didn't bother to go to school. She helped me make some investments, and we were able to have a better life. Before working at the law firm, she was a secretary at a dealership. They loved her there. She knew more than some of their head mechanics. Unfortunately, it became too overwhelming, so she quit."

"Wow, I didn't know mom had a passion for cars!"

"Well, let's pray that she makes it through and we can all began to heal and rebuild our relationships."

Alyce was happy to see that her dad was coming out of his depression phase, but he clearly wasn't being realistic about the next steps. Even if mom did fully recover, Grandpa James's side of the family wasn't going to allow her mother to live happily ever after. Surely, they would want a full-blown investigation and to see her mom prosecuted to the fullest extinct of the law.

Alyce paused for a minute. She thought about the fact that her dad said that mom and Grandpa James were having a heated argument before she stabbed him. Even the craziest person wouldn't stab their parent for helping to financially enable their grandchild, so what was the *real* reason behind the rage?

If Grandpa James was trying to attack her, she would have been frantic and called dad or the police for help. Alyce knew her mom, and she definitely wouldn't have waited three days later to say she was attacked. It also wouldn't make sense for her to try and kill herself if she was the victim.

Everything seemed so confusing and out of place. Alyce felt as if she was participating in the biggest prank of her life. Although her mom did slap her in the face a few months back, it never occurred to Alyce that her mom could stab and kill someone. It also never occurred to Alyce that her mom actually had a fetish for working on cars. It was such a manly job, which was the total opposite of the crafts she taught Alyce. Who was this woman that raised her all these years? Were the rumors about her having a half-brother actually true? What whole truth about grandma's accident did mom want to confess to her dad before she took the pills?

Alyce looked out the huge kitchen window and thought about everything. She thought about what possible scenario would cause mom to kill her own dad. Grandpa James was peaceful and charming. From the time she had been around and observed him, he wouldn't hurt a fly. Mom already had money and from the new information her dad gave her, she had plenty of it. Alyce stood there puzzled and conflicted until a grizzly thought finally came to her mind.

"Oh my God, dad, I think mom may have killed her mother."

Chapter 11

Her dad stood up and looked at her with an intense look of hurt and disappointment in his eyes. Alyce didn't intentionally mean to blurt out her private thought while her dad was in the room, but it slipped out, and there was no way to take it back. He was just starting to see the brighter side of things in his state of depression, so the last thing she wanted to do was to cause him even more mixed feelings. Even though she loved her dad, her thoughts and emotions had gotten the best of her. Hearing that mother worked on cars, then her grandmother was in a car accident at a time when they needed money sounded like a plot from the crime channel. On top of it all, her mom received a huge settlement, then disowned and later killed her own father. Alyce figured that Grandpa James must have discovered the secret and revealed that he knew the secret.

Alyce couldn't put together any other logical scenario. The thought that Grandpa James could have killed his wife did cross her mind, but that theory didn't make any sense. Why would her mom wait so long to get revenge and why wouldn't she and her grandmother's family members be persistent about seeing Grandpa James going to prison?

"What did you say?" Mr. Wilson asked.

"I... I was just thinking...would if...if mom's secret was something about her and grandmother? I mean...you said yourself that grandma was trying to stop mom's dreams, so-"

"You listen to me, Alyce," her dad demanded, walking close to her with an intimidating stare, "Your mother may have made some mistakes, but she is not a murderer! I don't want to ever hear you say anything else like that again! Do you understand?"

Alyce was so afraid she couldn't speak. A vein came across her dad's forehead as his nostrils began to flare. She'd never seen her dad so angry and defensive.

"Do you understand?" he firmly repeated

"Yes, dad," she softly responded, putting her head down as her dad walked out the room.

She instantly changed her mind about moving back home. She knew how much he loved her mom and would protect her at all cost. Even when her mom slapped her, her dad found a way to acknowledge her mother's positive attributes. With all this in mind, Alyce felt like if she stayed, her dad may resent her for her comment and perhaps even start to treat her differently. She refused to lose love from the person who she felt cared for her the most.

Alyce went to her bedroom and lied on her bed with tears in her eyes. This was definitely a serious conflict for her. Alyce felt as if her dad wasn't seeing the whole picture. Although she respected and loved her father, she had also grown to love Grandpa James as well. It wasn't fair for him to lose his life over unresolved issues that her mother allowed to fester. As much as she hated to think it, maybe it would be better if her mom didn't make it out of her coma.

"I'm going down to the hospital to check on your mother's condition. If she's not breathing on her own in a few days, the doctor said it's a possibility that she could become brain dead," Mr. Wilson sadly expressed, standing in the corner of Alyce's door.

Okay, dad. I hope she gets better soon. I'll definitely pray for improvements," she replied, feeling it was the right thing to say.

"Me too, kiddo, me too."

"Hey dad," Alyce called, just as he was walking off, "I'm sorry about accusing mom."

"It's okay, Sweetie. I apologize for how I reacted. It just brought back memories from years worth of old feuding in the past. It's a pretty good chance I'll be at the hospital overnight, so don't wait up. Sorry that this is how your first day home had to turn out."

After watching her dad leave in his most solemn state, Alyce closed her eyes hoping the day would just end. Feelings of guilt began to overcome her as she thought about how she wished she had never taken Grandpa James's money. Her mother wouldn't have had any reason to go visit Grandpa James. This was supposed to be the weekend where he was going to introduce her to more of her estranged family.

Just as she was about to wallow in an endless cycle of self-loathing, she received a phone call from Jasmine.

"Hello, Alyce? Are you there?" asked Jasmine, not hearing a greeting once the call became active.

Alyce struggled to hold back the trembling in her voice. "Uh...Jasmine, hi, how are you?" She finally replied, taking a deep breath.

"Is everything okay? You sound upset." Jasmine said, noticing the strain in Alyce's voice.

"Oh, it's nothing. Just some unexplained family things," Alyce stated, not wanting to graze the truth.

"Oh, I'm sorry to hear that. I hope everything works out."

"Thanks. I guess I'm just trying to work with the cards I was dealt."

"Well, I know this definitely may not be a good time, but," Jasmine paused as if she couldn't say what she wanted to say, "just try to call me as soon as you can, okay?"

Ironically, Alyce noticed an unsettling hesitation in Jasmine's voice as well. Jasmine knew Alyce would be spending time with family, so for her to call only a few hours after dropping her off at the airport also seemed strange. Although Alyce already had a lot on her shoulders, she knew something was wrong. She somehow felt it before the words even came out of Jasmine's mouth.

"Jasmine, what happened?"

"Alyce, I don't know how to tell you this, but...they...they found Kelsey."

"I knew she was going to get caught using that crap. Was she kicked out of school?"

There was another moment of silence from Jasmine's end of the phone. Alyce quickly realized she was underestimating the nature of what Jasmine had said. Tempted to hang up, she just held the phone.

"I'm sorry, Alyce. I didn't want you to find out that I knew and didn't tell you."

"Tell me what?"

"Oh Alyce, I'm so sorry," cried Jasmine

"Tell me what?" Alyce screamed.

Alyce could hear Jasmine still crying as she immediately hung up. Deep inside Alyce knew what was understood didn't need to be explained. She tried to separate herself from reality and pretend she didn't hear Jasmine or get the phone call altogether, but reality quickly set back in as soon as she saw her dad calling her. Shortly after, Kelsey's mom called. She didn't answer either call. She wasn't ready for the confirmation. Ultimately, she wasn't ready for death to happen to her again in the same day.

Not thinking rationally, Alyce ran across the hall to her mom and dad's room. She went into their master bathroom and opened the medicine cabinet. She saw several different painkillers, depression, and anxiety medications prescribed to her mom. Alyce knew her mom had had an overdose on something, but she was definitely unaware that her mother was taking so many different things. This discovery only added validation to Alyce's theory about her mom's involvement in her own mother's death.

It became obvious to Alyce that her mom was trying to suppress her guilt by self-medicating. It also made sense to why her mom had been so distant all these years. As Alyce continued to sort through her thoughts, she received a phone call from the last person she expected to hear from at the time. Once she didn't answer, she received a text begging her to please answer, so she instinctively changed her mind and answered.

"Jacob, you caught me at the worse time of my life, and I mean that literally. I can't even begin-"

"Alyce, I know who did it," interrupted Jacob.

Alyce was dumbfounded by his confession. "What do you mean you know who did it? You know who did what?"

"I... I think I know who killed Amanda and Kelsey."

Chapter 12

Alyce looked at her phone as if she saw Jacob literally coming through it. Was he even aware of what he was admitting and why was he admitting it to her? Better yet, was it true? Did this man really know what he said he knew? Why did he decide to tell her? Shouldn't he be at a police station giving a statement? Then another thought came to her. Would if he couldn't go to the police? Would if the person he was referring to was the man in the mirror? Alyce left the bathroom and sat on a lounge chair in her parents' room. She was already dealing with so much, so she knew she had to choose her next words very carefully. Jacob was obviously reaching out to her because he felt that she was someone he could trust. Whatever was going to come from Jacob's mouth, she knew she couldn't overreact. All she could do was hope that the man she had strong feelings for wasn't a killer.

"Are you at a place where you can talk about this?" Alyce finally asked.

"No, that's why I was calling you to see if we could meet up and talk."

"Oh my God, Jacob, I can't even begin to explain what's going on in my life right now."

"Listen, Alyce, I'm sorry. I know I've been distant lately, but I didn't know how to deal with tragically losing someone I once cared for while falling in love with a whole new person. A part of me felt like had I been there for Amanda, then maybe she would have had a chance. Then once I found out about Kelsey, I knew there wasn't anything I could do. Alyce, can we go somewhere and talk?

Once Alyce heard Jacob say that he found out about Kelsey, it slightly put her at ease regarding him being the killer. Jacob didn't sound aggressive or intimidating, but rather timid and fearful. Alyce clearly couldn't do anything about her mom's situation, but she could somehow help in this one.

"Well, I'm not on campus at the time. I came home for the break."

"Oh, when are you coming back?"

"I'm not sure. To be even more honest, I'm not sure if I'm coming back. I just found out today that my mom is in a coma and my dad is...he's going to need someone."

"Alyce, I'm sorry to hear that. Listen, I've saved up some money, so it wouldn't be a problem taking a flight down there if you need me."

"Jacob, you don't have to do that. Plus, you have school."

"I can catch a late flight and book a room for a few days. I promised you I would always be there for you and that's what I meant."

After a little more planning and convincing, Alyce finally agreed to Jacob's visit. Her mom was in a coma, she just found out her former best friend was murdered, and she no longer had Grandpa James. Since her dad was going to be spending most of his time at the hospital, Alyce was literally alone. Grandpa James's family probably was no longer even interested in meeting her because of what her mother did. She began to ponder how her wonderful life could come crashing down in an instance. Why should she have to suffer for her parents' and grandparent's demons? She came to the conclusion that her mom being strict on her and trying to instill on those bullshit values were a cover-up for her own wrongdoings. Alyce's thoughts continued to grow dark as she thought about all the sinister things she could and should have done. From then on, she decided she was no longer going to live under the perfect shadow of her mom that didn't exist.

A couple of hours later, Alyce received a phone call from Jacob letting her know that he had arrived at his hotel room. She was definitely ready to see him after finally speaking with her dad about Kelsey's death. Hearing him apologize repeatedly only made her recycle the memories from her last encounter with Kelsey. She needed comfort as well as a momentary escape. She needed someone to put their arms around her and at least say things would be okay. She still hadn't spoken to Kelsey's parents out of fear of what they may say or ask her.

She wasn't sure if Kelsey had already told them about the fight they had several weeks ago or the condition Kelsey was in when her body was found. She refused to be the one to reveal Kelsey's drug problem to people she knew and cared about since childhood. She wasn't even sure if she was going to attend Kelsey's funeral.

About thirty minutes later Alyce arrived at the Hilton and knocked on Jacob's door. He opened it and handed her a dozen of red roses.

"Hello beautiful, these are for you of course," he said, escorting her over to the table where another dozen of white roses set.

"First, I want to start off by saying I can't begin to imagine what you're going through. I won't try to pretend like I know how you feel because I don't know. What I do know is if there's anything you want or need me to do, I will do my best to make it happen. I'm all yours, and I'll never leave you hanging again."

"Thank you," Alyce replied, putting her flowers next to the others, so she could embrace him.

Alyce felt as if Jacob had read her heart and finessed her spirit. Those were the compassionate words she needed to hear. He felt so warm, and the cologne he had on was tantalizing. For the first time that she could remember, she felt sensual and desired. She wanted to stay in his arms forever. She didn't want to let go, and neither did he. He held her tighter and kissed her on top of her forehead as she pressed her body more firmly against him. He was totally unaware of the euphoria she was experiencing from the pill she had digested from her mother's medicine cabinet. She began softly kissing him on his neck as she slid her hands into his front pockets.

"Alyce wait," he said, holding her face up while looking deeply into her emerald green eyes, "as much as I would love to embrace this moment, I feel it's not the right time. I want your first experience to be special and under the right circumstances."

"Jacob, with everything that's going on, this may be the only night we'll have together for a while. I just need my mind, body, and spirit to wander off to a blissful moment in wonderland, even if it is for one night.

She didn't want to give him any time to object her proposition. She slowly began to unbutton his polo shirt, exposing his muscular chest and abs. She kissed his chest while pressing her hands firmly on his stomach, moving him backward towards the bed and climbing on top of him.

"Are you sure you've never done this," he teased.

"I'm not blind or deaf. I do watch and listen."

She let loose her pressed-out curls and pulled her oversized blouse over her head. He rose up, put one hand around her neck, and passionately kissed her on the lips. He moved his kisses downward towards her neck and caressed her breast through her bra. She felt a slight hesitation in his movements as if he was reconsidering what they were doing. She grabbed his hand and slid it inside her leggings. She could feel his arousal through his pants.

"Do you have protection?" she asked.

Jacob lifted his pelvis and pulled out his wallet. A few seconds later, Alyce phone began to ring. Trying not to spoil the moment, she chose to ignore the call, but the ringing continued.

"Maybe you should get that; it could be important."

Alyce got up from the bed and pulled her phone out of her purse.

"Alyce, you have to come up to room 412 right now! Your mom is in and out of consciousness, but she's specifically asking for you."

"Okay dad, I'll be right there."

"That was my dad. He said my mom is out of her coma and wants to see me."

"That's great, babe. I'll be right here waiting for your return."

"I was kind of hoping you could come with me."

"Babe, I would love to meet your parents, but I'm not sure if this is good timing."

"You don't have to come in with me. I just need your moral support."

Without another word, he fixed his clothes and handed her the blouse. He grabbed the room key and followed her to her car.

Once they arrived at the hospital, Alyce turned off the ignition and didn't move. She was feeling emotional and wasn't sure if she was ready for the visit. She quickly grabbed his hand and turned to him.

"It's going to be okay," he said, noticing the worry on her face.

"Jacob, I'm scared."

"What are you afraid of?"

"I haven't told you everything about my mom's coma. You see, my mom-"

Bang, bang, bang!

Alyce and Jacob were startled by a loud pounding on her driver's window.

"Are you really in the car with some hoodlum while your mother is on her deathbed!" Mr. Wilson yelled as Alyce rolled down her window.

"Well, shouldn't you be in there with her instead of standing outside trying to spy on me."

"Don't you take that tone with me, Alyce; I am not your mother!"

"I can't believe you of all people would try to embarrass me like this," she said, getting out of the car and slamming the door.

"You've clearly gotten out of control."

"You know something dad, ever since you told me what happened; you haven't once asked me how I feel about my mom trying to kill herself or the fact that she killed my grandfather. You've only been concerned with how this whole situation affects you. You should be thankful that this hoodlum has taken time from his job and college to be here for me."

Alyce walked toward the hospital entrance without looking back. She was ashamed that her dad would call someone he never met a hoodlum. Jacob was a very clean-cut type of guy, so her dad clearly wasn't referring to his attire. She never thought her dad would be the one to prejudge someone based on the color of their skin. Alyce was in tears before she even reached her mother's room.

"Are you the daughter?" A nurse asked, watching Alyce wipe her face as she stood by her mother's door.

"Uh, yes. I'm Alyce."

"Your mother has been in and out of it, but she's been asking for you."

Alyce slowly walked in and saw her mom hooked to several tubes. Her eyes were closed and it looked as if she was in a deep sleep. She had never seen her mom so helpless. As much as she wanted to turn around and head for the door, she knew she couldn't. She knew that there was a possibility that this could be the last interaction between them.

"Mom?" Alyce finally spoke.

Gloria blinked several times as her eyes slowly scoured the room. Once she looked in Alyce's direction, a look of horror crossed her face. Alyce looked back to see if someone was standing behind her, but they were alone.

"Glenda, I'm so sorry," Gloria softly cried, "Please forgive me. I didn't mean to do it."

Chapter 13

Alyce was very familiar with that name. She remembered Grandpa James using it frequently whenever he compared her facial features to her grandmother's face. He always said that Alyce and her grandmother, Glenda were about the same size and had the same crimson curls. Her mother must have been in some type of delusional state where she thought she was seeing her mom.

"You have to forgive me," she continued, "I was lost...I had nothing."

Alyce just stood there and watched her mother beg for forgiveness. She didn't know how to respond or if she should say anything at all. Should she pretend to be Glenda and try to get more information or should she try to wake her from her trance? Her mother had already said so much by saying so little. She wasn't sure if she was ready for a full confession.

"Why?" Alyce finally blurted out.

The room grew silent enough to hear a pen drop. Alyce had a sudden fear that her mom might have came to her senses from the recognition of her voice. She quietly stepped backward toward the door for a swift exit. She carefully placed her hand on the latch so she could inconspicuously slip out of the room.

"Danny threatened to leave," Gloria whispered, halting Alyce's escape. "You knew I couldn't take care of Charlie alone. You acted like I was a failure even after Charlie left. I was upset. I hated everything. I hated my life. I wanted to die. I wanted you to feel the pain I felt. Once I realized what I did, it was too late...I'm sorry mom, I'm so sorry. I need you to forgive me."

Alyce stood there paralyzed by what her mother was confessing. Although she didn't come out and say it, Alyce knew what her mother was implying. Watching her mom sob in desperation for her mom's forgiveness added more questions about what really happened. Did she rig her mother's car like Alyce expected she had? Who was Charlie and where did he go away to? What happened between her mother and Grandpa James that last fatal conversation? Just as Alyce was building up the courage to ask her questions, Gloria's whimpering turned into choking. Alyce moved closer to Gloria and noticed her eyes roaming toward the back of her head. Alyce thought she was having a seizure.

"Doctor!" Alyce yelled.

Gloria's heart rate machine started beeping as nurses rushed in forging Alyce to the side.

"Get her out of here," said one of the nurses as they continued to try and stabilize her mom.

After being pushed from her mother's room, Alyce stood against the wall beside the door. The truth was finally out. All that nonsense her father was telling her about her mom being mad because she couldn't become a mechanic was ludicrous. Mom wanted revenge because they made her give up her only son. The truth hurt Alyce deeply, but what hurt even more, was her dad lying to her.

A nurse saw Alyce and escorted her to the waiting room. After asking Alyce did she need anything, the nurse told her they would keep her updated on her mom's condition. A few minutes later, Alyce saw her dad jogging up the hallway towards her. She wondered did he have any clue that he was a major factor in her mom's treacherous scheme against his mother-in-law. For all she knew, her dad could have been in the plot. If mom was having trouble taking care of Charlie around the time of her mother's death, then dad would have known details about the mysterious Charlie.

"I heard the nurses paging Dr. Hines to room 412. How's your mother? Is she okay?" Mr. Wilson nervously asked, catching his breath while holding onto Alyce's shoulders.

"The nurse said it was routine," Alyce dishonestly responded, trying to get her questions answered first. "Who is Charlie?"

Mr. Wilson quickly took his hands down and stepped back. He must have realized that Gloria was the only one who could have given her that information. He turned around, put his head against the wall, and sighed.

"I don't think this is the right time or place to discuss this."

"Why?"

"It just isn't Alyce."

"Well, you know something dad, I think it is. I think it's about time you guys stop painting me a picture of rainbows and unicorns and tell me the truth."

"Your mom was pregnant with Charlie when I started dating her. She hid it from everyone, even me. Once your grandmother found out, all hell broke loose. She resented your mom for being pregnant out of wedlock and became verbally abusive toward her. Eventually, your grandmother convinced your mother to give Charlie up for adoption."

"Did my grandmother convince her or did you both convince her?"

"Alyce, why are you digging up issues from the grave when we're trying to keep your mother out of one?"

"Because you guys have been lying to me my entire life and the one person who was supposed to be here to protect me took away the only person that seemed to be genuine. I have a brother out there that I probably will never get the chance to meet for Christ sakes!"

"Excuse me, Mr. Wilson," a nurse interrupted, "we need you immediately."

As her father obediently followed the nurse, Alyce walked in the opposite direction and out of the hospital. She didn't want Jacob to see how upset and vulnerable she was, so she waited at the front entrance to dry her face. As she walked toward the car, she tried to figure out how she was going to explain her dysfunctional situation to Jacob. Although he was an understanding person, he may think that her mother's mental issues would be passed down to her. It made her reconsider telling him anything at all.

Alyce slowly opened the door and eased into the driver's seat. She could see Jacob staring at her in her peripheral vision but still wasn't sure if she should tell him the truth. She knew he wanted some type of update, but she didn't know what update to give him. If her mom survived the ordeal and she didn't tell him everything, how was she going to explain her mom is getting 25 years to life in prison? Her life was definitely going to end up being a feature on the crime channel.

"How did it go?" Jacob finally asked.

"Uh, she was in and out of consciousness, but she did apologize for what she did."

Alyce felt very proud and confident in her answer. She didn't have to lie, and she didn't have to tell him the whole truth.

"Do you think she's going to be okay?"

"I hope so," Alyce answered, not knowing if she meant it.

"Alyce, I want you to know that I'm not here to complicate your life any more than what you're already going through."

"Jacob, you are exactly who and what I need right now. I don't know if I'm making a mistake by admitting this to you, but you probably just saved my life."

"What do you mean?"

"Well, before you called me, I felt as if I had no one. My dad and I weren't seeing eye to eye; my mother was in a coma, and well…Kelsey," Alyce pause and looked at Jacob. With all the commotion going on and her coming down off of her high from her mother's opiates, she had almost forgotten that Jacob admitted to her that he knew Kelsey's killer.

"Jacob-"

"I know what you're going to say or ask me," Jacob interrupted, "so just give me a chance to explain."

Once again, Alyce knew this was probably going to be one of the most uncomfortable conversations she had to have. She was so caught up in trying to get to her family's truths that her mind had suppressed the fact that Kelsey was found slain. Although they were on bad terms, she hated the way that their childhood friendship had ended. Now, there was no way of reconciliation. She had to live with the fact that their last moments together were savage.

"I was devastated when Amanda got killed. To be even more honest with you, I still had feelings for her before she passed. I didn't know who to talk to, so I called Matthew. When I told him Amanda was dead, he said 'you owe me one' and continued talking as if everything was normal. I thought he meant I owed him because he exposed her and I let her go. Long story short, I went over to Matthew's house a couple of weeks later looking for a jacket that I let him borrow. Matthew wasn't home, so his aunt told me to go and look in his closet. Once I grabbed the jacket off of the top shelf, a folded paper with red marks fell on the floor. Being dumb and curious, I opened it."

"Okay, what was on it?" Alyce asked, eagerly waiting for the answer behind Jacob's sudden silence.

"It was a list of women in the nursing program. Four names were crossed out in red, including Amanda and Kelsey's name."

Chapter 14

"Jacob, this is crazy! Your cousin can't be a serial killer. I just met him a few months ago. I mean, serial killers are crazy people that were deprived, beaten, or raped as kids. Do you really think he did it?"

"I can't say for sure he did it, but he told me to thank him, and he has had a vendetta against nurses since he was a kid. Meredith, I mean Jacob's mother, had an in-house nurse once she was no longer able to be mobile. I actually had a little crush on the nurse when I was a little boy. She was a tall, slim lady with brunette hair and extremely white teeth with a smile that made me jittery. Matthew and I use to flip coins to see who would say hello to her first."

"Can we stick to the subject please?"

"Oh, sorry. Anyway, the day before Meredith died, her regular nurse called out for her scheduled shift, and the replacement nurse didn't either give her the right amount of pain medicine or the wrong medicine, I'm not really sure which one. Either way, Meredith passed away the following afternoon."

"Isn't that grounds for a lawsuit?"

"They tried that route, but the hospital had documents stating that Meredith was already in the final stages of her cancer, so she could have passed at any given time."

"Did the regular nurse feel bad or apologize for not showing up for work?"

"I don't think so. My mom told me that one of Meredith's closest friends, who worked as a nurse assistant, saw the nurse out partying the same night she was supposed to be taking care of Meredith. She reported the nurse, and they found marijuana in the nurse's system and fired her."

"That had to have been devastating for you guys."

"Yeah, I think everyone was looking for something or someone to blame. Matthew had it in his adolescent mind and heart that his mother was going to heal and be normal again, but after that incident, he blamed negligent nurses for his mother's death."

"Yeah, but do you really think he would go on a killing spree ten years later?"

At that moment, Alyce thought about what she had said. Here she was defending Matthew when her own mother just recently killed her father over a feud from almost 20 years ago. She couldn't comprehend how so much could happen in so little time. She definitely didn't want to believe that her boyfriend's cousin killed her childhood best friend.

"Are you thinking about turning him in as a suspect?" she asked.

"Would you turn in your family?" he countered back.

Although Jacob was clearly unaware of what was going on with her, his question rocked Alyce's spirit. Was she going to repeat to her dad what her mother said to her? Did the rest of her mom's family deserve to know the truth? Even if Grandma Glenda's death was an accident, Grandpa James death was very intentional. As much as Alyce didn't want to label it, her mom was a killer without a doubt.

"Like you said yourself, you don't go around accusing your loved ones over circumstantial information, right?" he asked.

"Right."

She realized that Jacob was just as lost as she was. He was looking for guidance that she couldn't give. Even if she wasn't dealing with her own family's criminal circumstances, how could she encourage Jacob to turn in his presumably guilty first cousin whose mom died of cancer. Besides, all Jacob had was a piece of Matthew's paper with red marks and his obnoxious response to Amanda's death. Perhaps he intended for Jacob to find the list. He did put it near Jacob's jacket. The more she thought about it, the more it sounded like Matthew wanted his cousin's attention. Perhaps she was Matthew's current nuisance.

"What do you want to do now?" Jacob asked.

"Well, I haven't really had an appetite all day, so I guess we could go grab something to eat."

The ride was silent as she tried to figure out the next steps in her life. She knew she didn't want to move back home with her dad. He would probably spend most of his time at the hospital or sulking all day, and she wasn't sure if she was ready to return back to campus

Once they arrived at the restaurant, Jacob immediately got out the car and opened the door for Alyce. He grabbed her hand and escorted her in as the hostess sat them at a table. After looking over the menu, Jacob ordered their food and excused himself to the bathroom. As Alyce sat at the table twirling her straw in her ice water, she noticed two women at the bar whispering and looking in her direction. Feeling slightly uncomfortable, she repositioned herself to where she was able to see the mounted flat screen television on the wall. Alyce almost fainted when she saw the headline TOP STORY: DAUGHTER ALLEGEDLY KILLS FATHER. Although the television was muted and they didn't show any photos, she figured it had to be a local news story about her mom. With her elbow on the table, she partially covered her face and waited for Jacob's return.

"We've got to get out of here," she whispered as soon as Jacob sat down.

"What do you mean? We haven't even eaten yet," Jacob reasoned.

"We have to get out of here now," Alyce demanded, slightly louder as she got up and walked off.

After falsely explaining to the waitress that Alyce had morning sickness, he took a final sip of water and followed behind her. Alyce ʳot in the car, put her head on the steering wheel, and accidentally ᵗhe horn.

ᵎlyce, what's wrong with you? Are you okay?"

ᵈid it! She did it, okay?" Alyce cried out.

ᵉ you talking about?"

"My mother killed her parents!"

"What?" he asked, not sure if he heard her correctly.

"My mom killed her mother and her father."

"Uh...I honestly don't know how to respond to something like that," he paused. "It's definitely extreme. Is there any particular reason you would say that?"

Alyce looked at him with tears in her eyes. She knew she would have to tell him the truth if she planned on being with him. He trusted her with his secret, so now it was time for her to confide in him.

"My mom stabbed and killed my Grandpa James, her dad. The morning she was supposed to turn herself into the authorities, she overdosed on opiates. A while ago, when I was in her room visiting her, she confessed it. She must've been out of her conscious mind because she thought I was her mother. She said it was too late to stop what she had done and begged for her mother's forgiveness."

Jacob leaned forward and wrapped his arms around her. He always seemed to know exactly what Alyce needed whenever she needed it. Alyce couldn't stop the tears from flowing and whimpered in his arms like a little baby.

"Whatever you want and need, I'm here for you."

"Let's just go back to D.C. I'll drive my car back, and we can park it at your place until next semester. I just want to get out of here," she pleaded, wiping her face.

"Uh...," he stalled as he took a deep breath, leaning his head toward the dashboard, "I'm not sure if that's the best idea right now."

"Why not?" She quickly questioned.

"Matthew had been blowing up my phone all day. When I finally got the chance to talk to him privately, he didn't answer. A few minutes ago, I went to the bathroom to see what he wanted."

"Well, what did he want?"

"He said he knew that I found the list and he needed it back."

"Wait, you took it?"

"I was nervous. I thought I heard his aunt coming, so I quickly stuck it in my pocket."

"So, what does this mean? Did he threaten you?"

"He asked me had I told anyone about it and I told him of course not. I couldn't tell if he believed me."

"Well, what did he say after that?"

"He wanted me to meet up with him. He said he was going on a vacation for a little while and he wanted me to come with him. When I asked him where; he said it was a surprise. I told him I came home with you to meet your parents and plus, I had work and school."

"Did he sound upset about your objections?"

"Not really. He suggested that I take off work for a few days and we could wait until my upcoming school break to go."

"Do you think it's a setup? I mean, is he capable of hurting you?"

"I don't think so. We've taken plenty of vacations together before. Maybe he wants me to think that everything is normal and he didn't do anything. Alyce, I honestly don't know. I've never been put in this type of predicament before."

"What did you tell him you were going to do after his suggestions?"

"I told him I would think it over and see what I could do."

"Are you considering going?"

"Absolutely not! He may be on the run. If he asked about the list, he has to assume that I think he did it. Especially with the comment he made about how I should thank him."

"Do you think that he thinks that you'll tell me?"

"If anything, he probably assumes I already told you, but wants to see where my loyalty lies. I'm not getting involved with killing anyone, and I'm definitely not willing to get you involved in this mess."

"Well, I'm kind of already involved. He knows that Kelsey was my best friend. Perhaps she discovered something about Amanda, and that's why he had to kill her. He may even think Kelsey confided in me about something."

"It sounds like a long stretch, but I'm not saying it's impossible. All I know is that I have to go somewhere for a while to escape the madness."

"What about your brothers and sisters?"

"They live in a different state, and I'm sure they don't know anything about what's going on at the moment, and I refuse to bring them into it."

"So, what should we do?" she asked.

"I have some money saved, and I plan to get out of town for a while. I know we've only been dating for a few months, but you're welcome to come with me. Matthew doesn't know where you stay, so you'll be safe here too if you didn't want to come. I'm just not sure if it's safe for you on campus."

"If he knew where Kelsey was from and where she lived, it wouldn't be hard to find out where I stay."

The car grew silent for a minute. The truth of the matter was that they were both in a tough predicament. Even without the Matthew and Jacob situation, Alyce knew she didn't want to move back home. On the other hand, she wasn't sure if she should move away with Jacob either. Although he seemed to be the perfect gentlemen, she didn't know any of his living habits. They hadn't even spent a night together. Alyce was in turmoil. She had less than a week to decide her fate.

Chapter 15

The next day, Alyce woke up in Jacob's room on the king-sized bed around 7:50a.m. She looked over to her side where Jacob was laying before she fell asleep, but he wasn't there. Her initial thought was that he went out to get breakfast, but she quickly remembered he didn't have a car. She reached for her purse on the table to retrieve her phone. She wanted to see if he had possibly left her message and didn't want to wake her. She didn't see a message, but she did notice five missed calls from her dad a few hours earlier. He didn't leave a voicemail, so she assumed that the calls weren't urgent. He probably went home, discovered she wasn't there, and wanted to know where she spent the night. She didn't feel like explaining where she was and she definitely didn't want a lecture. It was time for dad to understand that she wasn't a kid anymore, so all the lies and fairy tales in wonderland were over. Besides, she wasn't quite sure if she was ready for the update on her mom's condition, she decided to return his call later.

She got up, walked around the corner, and discovered that Jacob had let out the sofa bed. It was at that moment that Alyce was reassured that he was a true gentleman. She didn't want to wake him, so she went into the bathroom to freshen up her face. Shortly after turning the water off, she heard shuffling in the other room. She knew Jacob was awake, so she gave her hair one last tweak before leaving the mirror. She stepped out and saw him making coffee on the counter.

"I didn't know you were a coffee person," she said, walking in his direction.

"Uh, actually I'm not. I just figured we both could use some since we didn't get a lot of sleep."

"How long did you stay up after me?"

"Probably about an hour or so. Matthew called a few times, but I didn't answer. He sent me a message saying he guesses he knows who I chose."

"Is he always like that when you meet a girl?"

"Well, Amanda was the first girl I had really been serious with, so I guess there aren't any other situations to compare."

"Oh...well, I was going to run home, take a shower, and maybe we can talk over breakfast."

After he agreed, Alyce received a soft kiss on her forehead. She left the room with butterflies in her stomach. She was amazed by the way he made her feel even in controversy. On her drive home, she decided she wasn't going to tell her dad that she spent the night with Jacob. It was easier for her to say that she stayed over at a friend's house and grieved over Kelsey.

Alyce took a deep breath as she opened the garage door. Even though she had her story planned out, she still felt overwhelmed about lying to her dad. Although her mother had deceived her, she still loved and respected her dad. Alyce knew that her dad was a stooge and her mom masterminded everything. She felt that anything her dad had lied to her about was coerced by her mother.

Much to her surprise, her dad wasn't there. Perhaps he had gone back to the hospital, or maybe he hadn't been there at all. When she entered the house, the lights were off, and the kitchen was still spotless. Alyce went ahead and showered so she could avoid seeing her dad and get back to Jacob. This would prevent her from having to lie to his face about not returning his calls and explaining where she was on her way to this morning. She also grabbed more clothes and personal items for her journey of uncertainty.

All packed up, Alyce was about to head back to Jacob's room. Her heart nearly fell out of her chest when she heard the garage door open. She quickly put her things in her closet and pretended like she was watching television. She started flicking through the channels as she heard walking towards her room.

"Hi, sweetie," he said, in a chipper but nervous way.

"Hi, dad," she replied, embracing his hug.

"I called you earlier to tell you the great news."

"Yeah, I kind of slept in this morning."

"I thought so. Listen, Alyce; I want to apologize for being so hard on you lately. I was so afraid of losing your mother; I wasn't thinking with a straight head. I also want you to apologize to your friend for me. I was out of line and wrong for the name calling."

"Uh, okay. What's the good news?" Alyce asked.

"Your mother started breathing on her own earlier this morning! Isn't that fantastic?"

"Of course, dad," Alyce responded, faking a burst of happiness.

"Listen, I know a few things will have to change, and we'll have to make some adjustments, but what's important is that we're going to be a family again."

"Aren't you worried that mom may go to prison?"

"Alyce, your mom is not a suspect."

"Dad, I saw it on the news."

"You must have seen something else. No one knows that your mom visited James."

"She told us."

"No, she told me, and I told you."

"What are you saying, dad?"

"What I'm saying is to let me handle the business side of things regarding your mom, and you focus on building your relationship with her. Besides, with Kelsey passing I know there's a lot on your plate. I thought maybe you could even take a semester off from school to help with your mom while I'm at work."

"Kelsey didn't pass, dad, Kelsey was murdered."

"Yes, but that's the other news I had to tell you. I got wind that the police apprehended two suspects in the case."

"What? Did you find out the names of the suspects?"

"No, honey, but they have strong leads-"

"Were they working together, or is it two separate investigations?" Alyce interrupted, unable to contain her emotions."

"Sweetie, I don't know, but what I do know is that this situation isn't easy to deal with and I'm sorry what you're going through. I'm just trying to be here for you."

"Are you, dad? Because Kelsey isn't the only person, I lost. Despite how you guys felt, I loved Grandpa James."

"I'm not doubting or questioning your feelings. What I'm saying is that we are all we got and there shouldn't even be a question about whether or not to turn in your mom.

"What happens when the investigators start looking up phone records and asking questions?"

Her dad quenched his eyes and turned up his lips as if he hadn't thought of that. Alyce watched him put his hands in his pocket and look out the window. He always gave the same blank stare whenever he was trying to come up with a plan or solution for something. He was so caught up in protecting his wife that he wasn't concerned for her safety or the fact that there now may be two killers around her campus. He acted as if his only reason for breathing was her mom. Alyce decided that she wasn't going to compete for his attention.

"I'm going to pack some more things and head back to campus since mom is doing better. I'm also going to register my car, so I'll have it for next semester."

"Do you think that's the best thing to do right now with all that's going on?"

"Yes, dad, I do."

"Okay, angel. If you feel that's the better decision for you, I have to support it. Just be safe and let me know if you change your mind about staying home."

After getting her belongings from her closet, her dad helped her pack her things in the trunk. She hugged her dad tight and told him she would try to make it home for the holidays. A part of her felt like her dad wanted her to leave since she was against the idea of pretending as if her mother was innocent. Knowing what her mother had done only complicated their already strained relationship. Not only could she not live with her, but it may be quite some time before she could face her.

Once Alyce got back to Jacob's room, she anxiously knocked on his door. She wondered did he get the same news as her dad did and was Matthew one of the suspects. She could definitely tell something was wrong by the look on his face when he opened the door.

"What's going on, babe?"

"I think you need to sit down for this," he suggested.

"My dad mentioned that two guys were arrested for Kelsey's murder," Alyce mentioned, thinking that's what he wanted to talk about.

"Alyce, Matthew called me from a pay phone about thirty minutes ago and told me he was leaving town immediately. He said he led police on a false trail to buy time until I got back. When I told him, I wasn't coming with him, he went in maniac mode."

"So, he is admitting it was him! Well, what else did he say?" Alyce asked, feeling like he was omitting details.

"It's not important. I'm not leaving you, and that's final. Let's go get us some breakfast."

"Since he is leaving, we could just continue our lives in D.C, right?"

Jacob put his head down. "I wish it was that simple. Matthew is unpredictable. Don't get me wrong, he's always been a bit of a rebel, but this is a side of him I've never known. It's not a good idea for either of us to go back right now."

"Why, did he threaten you?"

"Alyce, just trust me on this one, okay?"

"Jacob, you keep giving me all these warnings, but you're leaving out the reason for the warnings?"

He grew silent. He looked at her with tears in his eyes as he grabbed her hand and held it.

"He said he needs you out of the picture."

"I'm sure those are your choice words. What did he really say?"

"It doesn't matter. I'm never going to let anyone hurt you."

The look in his eyes told her that he meant it, which made Alyce almost immediately fall in love. She felt safe with him. Her dad couldn't protect her from her mom, and without Jacob, no one could protect her in D.C. She felt her only logical decision was to go with Jacob. She wasn't sure where he planned to go, but she hoped he had some kind of a plan.

"Since I can't stay here and we both can't go back to school, what will we do?"

"I talked to my Uncle Greg. He's my mother's brother who lives in Chattanooga, Tennessee. He is the senior operation manager at a chemical factory, and he said he could get me a job starting off at about $38,000 a year without a degree. He said once I finished school; he could get me a supervisor position."

"That sounds great, but where will we live and what would I do?"

"They have great schools there. You can tell the University's administration department that you have to withdraw due to a family emergency. That way, you can keep your scholarship and start somewhere else next semester."

"Do you think that Matthew would find us?"

"No, Uncle Greg was in the Marines, so he lived overseas since he was 19. He never even met my dad. He relocated about two years ago after his divorce, but my mom was the only sibling he kept in touch with after my grandfather died. As far as anyone else is concerned, he still lives overseas. He has a few duplexes that he rents out, or we could stay in his pool house until we find our own place."

"What about your dad? Since he is Matthew's blood uncle, do you think he would say anything to Matthew's dad?"

"Matthew's dad split when his mom first got sick. He hasn't heard from him since he was 11. My dad has Alzheimer's disease. He can barely remember his own name."

"Oh, I'm sorry to hear that."

"It's okay. No one likes to talk about it, but it doesn't take away from the great dad he has been to us. He knows who we are most of the time even though he doesn't always remember our names," Jacob added, trying to crack a smile in his solemn moment.

"Well, I guess the decision is made. We will journey to Tennessee."

After going out for breakfast, Alyce decided that Jacob should drive as they headed back to Washington together. This gave her time to write an official withdrawal letter to submit to the University. Since she knew she wouldn't have time to sit and talk to Jasmine, she wrote her a letter as well. It stated how much she appreciated their friendship and thanked her for her beautiful spirit. She was cautious about putting details of her departure in the letter, so she plainly explained that she had to move away due to a family emergency. She promised to always keep in contact with her and that she would text her once she reached her destination.

After a spontaneous four-and-a-half-hour drive, Alyce went directly to the admissions office where she dropped off her letter and briefly spoke with a counselor. She then went to her room to pick up her belongings. Jasmine wasn't there, so she left the note on her bed. She looked around the room before slowly walking out of the door. It was a quick and somber ending to what she thought was her new beginning.

They headed to Jacob's home after leaving the university. Their plan was to get Jacob's truck, gas up both vehicles, and head out for the open road. After about ten minutes into the drive, Alyce heard sirens and horns in the distance and started to get an eerie feeling. She put in mind that it was just a routine occurrence of firefighters or paramedics doing their jobs. She noticed that Jacob was moving closer and closer to the sounds as he drove. A few minutes later, she saw smoke. She also became aware of the worrisome look that began to form on Jacob's face. A few minutes later, her intuition was confirmed.

Jacob pulled up to a duplex that was blocked off by police cars and fire trucks. His home was engulfed in flames. Jacob immediately jumped out of the car and started running toward the duplex, but the firemen grabbed him. Alyce immediately followed him.

"Did you get the family next door out?" Jacob yelled.

"Calm down, sir. What is your name?" An officer asked.

"No, a little girl and boy lived next door. Are they safe?" Jacob screamed a little louder.

"Calm down sir, or we'll have to detain you," repeated the officer.

A few seconds later a slim, blonde lady came running up to Jacob and hugging him. She explained that her husband and kids weren't home, and she had just gotten the call from her sister who owned the unit. Jacob was relieved as he almost fell to the ground.

After about an hour, the fire had completely subsided, and investigators took pictures. A lead fireman walked up to the tenants and explained that the opposing unit had a little smoke damage, but the majority of Jacob's side was toast. Luckily, Jacob packed most of his important items and took them with him on his trip to see Alyce. They permitted him to go in and salvage anything that he could.

Alyce grabbed his hand as they slowly walked toward the torched unit. The living room had minimal damage, but everything surrounding it looked like a scene from a horror movie. Jacob didn't smoke, and he hadn't cooked in weeks. He knew that someone maliciously started the fire. Jacob immediately escorted Alyce back to her car as the officers pulled him to the side for questioning. A few minutes later, he returned with a contact card.

Once Jacob got back in the car, he put his head on the steering wheel. In her mind, Matthew was the only one who would be capable of such a heinous crime, but she wasn't going to comment on her suspicion. Not knowing what to say; she gently placed her hand on his shoulder and rubbed his arm. After a few minutes, he turned to her and gave her a half smile.

"Sometimes you have to go through hell in order to get a piece of Heaven." he said.

With that statement, he kissed her on her lips and got in his truck. She followed him to the gas station prior to making their nine-hour trip to Chattanooga as planned. Even with all they had been through in so little time, Alyce was optimistic about their new journey. As she sat in her car watching Jacob pump her gas in her rearview mirror, she knew she was making the right decision. Jacob showed her that he was everything she could want in a man. He was caring, supportive, ambitious, and thoughtful. She felt as if he possessed a lot of the good qualities that her dad had. She quickly wiped the single tear that was falling down her face from the reality of leaving her dad.

After he was finished, Jacob came around to the driver's side to make sure Alyce was ready to take the drive. He handed her a pack of caffeine pills just in case she felt herself feeling tired. He told her he didn't mind camping out at a hotel if she started feeling drowsy. She assured him that she was okay and they kissed once more before getting ready to leave. Jacob input the directions on his GPS and called his uncle to let him know that they were leaving out. Just as Jacob was about to head out, he received a text.

Matthew: I think I've proved my point by showing u that choosing her over me was a BIG mistake that you'll live to regret

Thank you for your purchase; I sincerely hoped you enjoyed your read. For more interesting novels, guides, and e-books visit

www.imadethebook.com

Acknowledgements
Cori Lawhorn